Fire
WITCH

Books by Matt Ralphs

Fire Girl
Fire Witch

Fire
WITCH

MATT RALPHS

MACMILLAN CHILDREN'S BOOKS

First published 2016 by Macmillan Children's Books
an imprint of Pan Macmillan
20 New Wharf Road, London N1 9RR
Associated companies throughout the world
www.panmacmillan.com

ISBN 978-1-4472-8357-7

1 3 5 7 9 8 6 4 2

A CIP catalogue record for this book is available from
the British Library.

Printed and bound by CPI Group (UK) Ltd, Croydon CR0 4YY

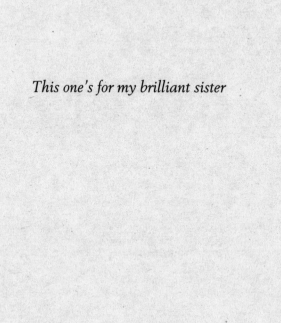

This one's for my brilliant sister

CONTENTS

Hath not the present Parliament
A ledger to the demons sent,
Fully empower'd to treat about
Finding revolting Witches out?

Hudibras by Samuel Butler

PROLOGUE

London, England, 1656

Matthew Hopkins, the Witch Hunter General, offered his prisoner a friendly smile. 'Well, Nicolas?' he said. 'Don't you want to come outside? Breathe God's fresh air?'

Ragged, pale, stooped in chains, Nicolas Murrell emerged blinking on to the roof of Cromwell Tower. A warm summer breeze blew the prison shadows away, and for a heartbreaking moment he let his mind soar free.

How long have I been here? he thought. *Three days? Three weeks?*

It felt like forever.

Not long ago he had been a feared outlaw and demonologist leading a coven of witches against the Order of Witch Hunters. But now his plans were nothing but ashes in his mouth, and all he had to look forward to was a slow death at the hands of Hopkins, his bitterest enemy.

Murrell stood tall. *I am not afraid.*

'Clank, clank, clank.' Hopkins smiled, taking Murrell's

1

arm and leading him down the flagstone path.

Trellissed roses engorged the air with perfume; bees droned among the petals, sun-drunk and greedy for pollen.

'You've been my guest at the Tower for a month and have yet to speak a single word,' Hopkins said with a shake of his head.

As he walked Murrell stole a glance at his captor. A comfortably lived middle age had softened his face – but his eyes, oh yes, they were as hard as ever.

'Such a shame, because old acquaintances like us have so much to talk about.' Hopkins paused to pinch a rose from its stem and let it fall. 'Diseased. *Rotten.*' He crushed it under his boot. 'Like so much else in this world.'

On they went until they emerged into a perfectly manicured garden of raised flower beds basking in the sun. Sprays of poppies, bursts of marigolds, swollen, heart-shaped tulips – red everywhere Murrell looked. Red. *Blood-red.* The colour of Hopkins' murderous Order.

'Welcome to my respite,' Hopkins said. 'Beautiful, isn't it?'

Murrell hid his queasiness behind a blank stare. Far below spread London, her rooftops, towers and spires shimmering under a heat haze.

This monstrous Tower rises higher than every building in the city, he thought. *It must be visible from miles around.*

'I tend my garden and it repays me with beauty and colour.' Hopkins gestured around him. 'And in that spirit I keep you safe from those clamouring for your execution, yet you give me nothing in return. Whatever happened to *quid pro quo?*'

The sun glowered down like a swollen eye. Murrell blinked and sweated. *I am not afraid*, he thought. *I am not . . . afraid.*

'I already know a lot,' Hopkins continued, plucking out a thorn that had embedded itself in his finger. 'David Drake, that Witch Finder's boy you tangled with, he's told us what you and your Coven were doing at Rivenpike. Tut, tut! Consorting with demons and practising black magic to try and overthrow my beloved Order? Still, old habits, eh, Nicolas?'

Murrell watched as a robin with a lame leg tucked into his feathers hopped out from a nearby hedge. Was he mistaken, or was the little bird watching him back?

'Drake is cooperating.' Hopkins licked the blood from his finger. 'If only you would do the same – it would make our lives *so* much easier.'

The robin hopped closer, head cocked, black eyes shining.

'You're probably wondering why I've not been *administering* to you in the usual ways this time,' Hopkins said with a smile. 'Well, I tried that before and it got me nowhere. Even when I –' he imitated a pair of scissors with his fingers – 'snipped bits off you. It seems like a long time ago now, doesn't it? Do you remember?'

Murrell felt an itch where his thumb used to be. He remembered. He remembered that night very well.

3

'So I've decided to take a more radical approach to our situation. This way, please.' Butterflies swarmed around Hopkins as he set off down another path; for a precious moment he disappeared from view.

Seizing his chance, Murrell picked the unresisting robin up and felt a warm connection between them. Giddy with relief, he recited some magic words then whispered, 'Greetings, my new friend. Will you be a quick and secret familiar for me? Will you help me escape this prison?'

'I will,' the robin replied with a soothing pulse of magic. 'My name is Thorn, and you are not alone any more.'

'Thank you,' Murrell breathed, letting the robin flutter away. 'Thank you . . .'

Hopkins was waiting for him by a low metal hatch built into the battlements. At his signal, two soldiers appeared seemingly from nowhere and grabbed Murrell's arms.

'I call this the Oven,' Hopkins said, wrenching the hatch open. 'It used to be a coal scuttle, and as you can see it's quite small.'

Quite small? Murrell thought. *It's tiny! Surely he doesn't mean . . .* Fear stole his breath as he realized what Hopkins was about to do.

Hopkins poked his head into the darkness. 'Goodness, it's like a furnace in here!' He re-emerged with a smile and nodded to the guards, who tightened their grip around Murrell's neck and thrust him through the hatch.

The confines forced him to tilt his head to one side and draw his knees up to his chin. He gasped. Where there should have been air there was only heat, prickling his scalp and scouring his throat.

'You can cooperate,' Hopkins said, 'or you can roast. It's your choice.'

The last thing Murrell saw before the hatch clanged shut was the Witch Hunter General picking up a snail from the path and tossing it over the battlements.

1
FIRE MAGIC

Hazel opened her heart and let the magic loose. Fire washed through her, heating her blood. She breathed in brimstone, feeling powerful, feeling *dangerous*.

Titus's words echoed through her mind: *You must understand your magic, and learn how to control it.* Planting her feet further apart, she adjusted her balance as the fire inside intensified. Her heart raced, each beat booming into the next, faster and faster.

I'm a Wielder, she thought. *A Fire Witch, and I am in control.*

The moon was only a sickle in the sky, but the forest clearing lit up bright as day when Hazel engulfed herself in a blazing cocoon of magic. Firelight burnished the trees and shimmered through the leaves.

She focused on a dark figure standing twenty paces away – tall, crooked and with a swollen, misshapen head. A demon, a monster, an enemy to be burned . . . The flames roared louder as she willed them into a swirling ball around her left fist.

Aim for the head . . .

Placing her weight on to her back foot, Hazel cocked her arm, swivelled, and with a grunt of effort hurled the fireball in one smooth motion. It raced away, a yellow comet trailing smoke, and she knew straight away that she'd got it wrong.

Too much force . . . It's going to . . .

The figure smashed backwards into a tree and exploded in an eye-scorching flash. Hazel covered her face against the blast. By the time she looked up the fire had dissipated, leaving behind the smell of smoke and a few smouldering patches of grass. She sank to her knees, shaking with exhaustion.

A man in a long black coat emerged from behind a tree and grimly surveyed the devastation. 'Oh yes,' he said. 'Well done. Very controlled.'

'I'm sure no one in a ten-mile radius saw *that* little display,' the dormouse perched on his hat added.

Hazel stood up, smoothed the wildness out of her deep red hair with all the dignity at her disposal and snapped at the mouse: 'Bramley, I'm really not in the mood for your sarcasm. And Titus, I'm doing my best, aren't I?'

'Your best isn't good enough,' the old man said as he strode up to her. His name was Titus White, and Hazel had employed him to help find her mother after she had been kidnapped by the demonologist, Nicolas Murrell. 'You've been practising wielding for weeks and you're still hopeless.'

Bramley, Hazel's closest friend and magical familiar,

jumped on to her shoulder and buried himself in her hair.

'I hit the targets now,' Hazel said hotly. 'Every time.'

'Yes, and every damn thing around them.' Titus picked up the smoking remains of the scarecrow and threw it on the pile with the others she'd immolated that night. He snapped his fingers. 'Come with me, girl.'

Hazel kicked at the ground and followed him to the edge of the clearing. Dusky fields and forests sloped down towards a vast constellation of twinkling lights.

'Look down there,' Titus said. 'That's London. We'll be there tomorrow, and if anyone gets the slightest whiff of your magic then you and me both will be arrested and sent to the pyres.'

'I never asked you to come with me,' Hazel said, folding her arms. 'You *insisted*.'

'Yes, because your mother would have wanted me to,' Titus said. 'And I'll do right by her or slit my own throat.'

'So what are you complaining about then?'

'I'm complaining because I know she'd want me to stop you from pursuing your plan to rescue her.'

'I can't leave her in Baal's clutches – who knows what torment that demon is putting her through?' A ripple of fire ran through Hazel's hair. 'I'm getting her back, Titus, and you can't stop me.'

'I can lock you in a chest,' he growled.

Hazel glared at him. 'Just you try! I'll burn my way out.'

'Damn it all, girl, can't you listen to reason? Murrell is the Order's prisoner. For all we know he might already be dead.

And even if by some miracle you do get to speak to him, why would he help you, the girl whose interference got him arrested in the first place?'

'I don't know, but I'm going to try anyway.' Hazel stomped back into the clearing. 'Stay here if you want – I don't need your help.'

'And what about Bramley?' Titus called after her. 'Does he get a choice about the peril you're dragging him into?'

Titus's huge horse Ajax was tethered to a tree. Hazel stopped to run her hand down his nose. 'I'm doing the right thing,' she murmured, and as if sensing her doubt the faithful old stallion gave her a gentle nuzzle.

Leaving him to his grass, Hazel climbed into the enclosed wagon that she and Titus called home. The one-room interior, complete with bunk beds, table and workbench, was its usual wondrous mess. Books, maps and strange mechanical devices lay scattered over every surface. A stove glowed contentedly with a pan of milk simmering on top.

Hazel breathed deeply, feeling some of her anxiety fall away; the wagon had been her home for the past few weeks and she'd grown to love it.

'You're very quiet, Bram,' she said, plucking her tiny familiar from her hair and holding him in the palm of her hand.

'I'm tired,' Bramley said irritably, trying to scrabble back up into Hazel's tangled red locks. 'I've only had three naps today.'

'You understand why I'm going to London, don't you?'

Hazel said, lifting him to eye level. 'Every second Ma spends trapped in the Underworld, it *hurts* me. I feel it in my heart, a sort of wrenching and twisting. I have to try and save her, and I need you—'

'To help,' he finished, hopping on to the table. 'It's all right, Hazel, I want to. You're my witch, so where you go, I go too.'

Before she had a chance to ask if he really meant it, Titus threw open the door and stormed inside. 'That's right, girl, keep running away. It's easy to ignore the brutal truth if you refuse to look it in the eye, isn't it?'

'The truth?' Angry magic fizzed through Hazel's hair. 'Is that what you want? Then how about this for a dose? You're a washed-up drunkard, Titus White, and it's your neglect that drove your apprentice away to side with the Witch Hunters.'

'And it was you that nearly got him killed by that spider-demon!' Titus bellowed, making a lunge for her.

Hazel darted behind the table, gathering an apple-sized ball of magic between her hands. Ensuring it was not hot enough to hurt, she threw it at Titus's chest. Surprised, he cried out and fell backwards into a chair.

Before either of them could land another blow, either verbal or physical, Bramley let out a warning flash of his own fire magic. 'Can you two please, for once, just try to get along?' he squeaked. 'Hazel – although Titus has many faults and bad habits, he's our friend and we need his help.'

'But—' Hazel began.

'Hush!' Bramley turned to Titus. 'Titus – Hazel is stubborn and will do whatever she wants no matter what we say. So we may as well rub along together and get on with it, hadn't we?' His whiskery frown deepened. 'Hadn't we?'

Hazel's anger was already slipping away. She knew blaming Titus for David's betrayal wasn't fair. After all, she was the one who had employed the two of them to help find her mother, so the trouble they had got into since was all down to her.

'You know, Hazel,' Titus said, patting himself down to check for injuries, 'I thought I'd hate it when Bramley decided he was going to talk to me as if he were my familiar, but he does occasionally speak sense.'

'I suppose he does sometimes,' Hazel admitted. She took Titus's hand and helped him up.

'Your aim's improved,' he said, brushing off his coat.

Hazel shrugged. 'I suppose it depends on how angry I am with the target.'

Titus's mouth twitched with a smile. 'And your magic – it was cold.'

'I wanted to hit you, not burn you alive.' Hazel looked away. 'Sorry,' she mumbled.

'Friends again?' Bramley said, climbing into his favourite teacup and yawning mightily. 'Good.'

Titus sat down at the table and began to clean out his pipe bowl. Hazel poured them both some warm milk from the stove and sank down on to her bunk.

'So, we'll be in London tomorrow?' she said.

'Aye. We'll leave the wagon here and ride the rest of the way on Ajax. If David really is working with the Witch Hunters he's most likely told them all about us, so we need to travel incognito.'

'Huh! David . . .' Bramley said. 'Nasty little turncoat.'

Hazel stared into the milk. David Drake, Titus's former apprentice. Brave, courteous and handsome – at least he had been until Spindle the spider-demon had poisoned him and cost him an eye. *My fault*, she thought. *Not Titus's. Mine.*

The three companions sat in silence for a while as the leaves outside hissed like shingle on a beach.

'Your mother would want me to stop you, you know,' Titus said.

'I know.'

'But I can't, can I?'

Hazel didn't look up. 'No.'

Titus sighed and put his pipe back in his pocket. 'It's no wonder I'm driven to drink.'

'I need your help,' Hazel said softly. 'I really can't do this without you.'

'I'm still here, aren't I?' Titus tossed a blanket over her head. 'Now get some sleep, you foolish witch. For who knows what tomorrow will bring?'

'Trouble, that's what,' Bramley muttered from his teacup. 'And strife.'

2
AT THE GATES

*'I resolved to go to London, the theatre
of all my misery to come.'*
Joseph Cotton (died of plague in 1655)

'Well, there it is,' Titus said, drawing Ajax to a halt on the brow of a sunlit hill. 'London.'

Hazel lifted herself up in the saddle and peered over his shoulder. 'Oh *my* . . .'

A city covered the valley floor, brown and hazy under the smoke from fifty thousand chimneys. Church spires, towers and temples pierced the rooftops, and through the middle of it all looped a wide grey river. Tenements and warehouses lined the north bank, leaning forward as if struggling to hold back the crush of buildings behind them.

Hazel shook her head in wonder. 'It's the most amazing thing I've ever seen.'

'It stinks, even from here,' Bramley squeaked from the brim of her hat.

'He's right. The place is a cesspit,' Titus said, urging Ajax onward.

They followed a lane along the edge of the forest until it joined a cobbled road heaving with traffic: farmers drove livestock, traders pushed handcarts, and pedlars with bulging panniers slung over their shoulders shouted out their wares. All were heading to London.

Titus urged Ajax into the flow behind a swaying hay wain. Hazel hardly knew where to look; she had never seen so many people before. *I wonder if any of them are witches, keeping their powers secret like me?* Bramley, who disliked noise, buried himself in her hair.

Titus bought a pie from a hawker on the side of the road and handed it to Hazel. 'Remember – we run a rat-catching business, I'm Mr Arthur Lowe, and you're my daughter, Demelza.'

'Why do I have to have such a silly name?' Hazel said through a mouthful of pastry.

'I had a dog called Demelza once, so it'll be easy for me to remember.'

Bramley stirred mischievously behind her ear. 'You *do* look like a Demelza. It suits you.'

'We're nearly at the gate,' Titus said. 'Make sure your rat stays hidden.'

'How *dare* you!' Bramley squeaked. 'I'm a *dor*mouse, and—'

'Hush, Bram,' Hazel said. 'You can scold him after we're inside. For now just stay out of sight.'

The wheat fields and pastures came to an abrupt halt at the foot of a gigantic earthwork wall, a remnant from the Witch War encircling the whole of London. The wooden parapets were long-gone and grass now grew on its slopes, but the stone-fortified gate ahead was still a formidable defence.

Soldiers wearing lobster-pot helmets interrogated everyone before letting them pass, and Hazel's heartbeat quickened as they edged closer; she felt horribly conspicuous, as if her magic was plain for all to see.

'Here we go,' Titus muttered as one of the soldiers beckoned them over with his billhook.

'State your business,' he said.

'I'm Arthur Lowe, a rat-catcher from Bristol,' Titus said, affecting a West Country burr.

The soldier turned his keen gaze on to Hazel. 'And you?'

'Lizzie Lowe,' Hazel said. 'Apprentice rat-catcher and company bookkeeper.'

'Rat-catchers, eh?' The soldier frowned. 'Where're your cages? Haven't you got any ferrets?'

'My brother's following later with our gear,' Hazel replied.

The soldier grunted. 'Off your horse, the both of you. I need to check you for plague signs.'

'But we're fit as fleas,' Titus said amicably. 'No plague on us.'

'Are you going to cause me trouble?' The soldier hefted his billhook.

'No, sir,' Hazel said, jabbing Titus in the ribs. 'We're happy to help.'

She dismounted and allowed the soldier to tip her head back with his gloved hand and examine her neck for buboes;

16

it was clear he was reluctant to touch her in case she was infected.

'You seem all right,' he said after checking them both. 'But if you want to stay plague-free be careful where you go. Southwark's rife with it, so be warned.'

'That's why we're here,' Titus said, remounting Ajax and helping Hazel up behind him. 'We'll soon get rid of the vermin—'

'Vermin ain't the cause,' the soldier said. 'It's those filthy witch prisoners the Order has penned up on the river.'

'Oh, aye? Many of them, are there?'

'Hundreds. Locked up in a prison hulk and breathing foul vapours everywhere. They're the cause of this outbreak, mark my words.'

'Burn the lot of them, I say,' Hazel said, tasting the ugliness of the words.

'Beats me why they don't! Hopkins ain't doing the job he's paid for . . .' The soldier trailed off. 'Well, I think I've said enough. On you go.'

'Much obliged to you,' Titus said, tipping his hat as he urged Ajax on.

'Think fast, girl!' the soldier called as he lobbed a pear at Hazel, who caught it one-handed.

'Thanks!' she called back.

'I said your name was Demelza,' Titus said as they entered the gatehouse.

'My name, my choice.' Hazel polished the pear on her dress. 'And I prefer Lizzie – after Queen Elizabeth Tudor.

You told me she liked witches.'

'Yes, well, things are different now, so have a care. The Witch Hunters will be looking for us, so keep the story straight and your magic hidden.'

'And that means controlling your temper,' Bramley added.

'Stop nagging, the both of you,' Hazel said. 'I'm the most even-tempered person you could ever wish to meet.'

'If that's the case, we're doomed,' Bramley groaned.

3
THE BANNERED MARE

*Southwark is an abominable sink of
beastliness and corruption.*
The Prudent Traveller *by Gerhardt Ohler*

Southwark High Road struck a straight line between handsome timbered houses all the way to London Bridge and the Thames. It was market day, and a swirling sea of people flowed around stalls and handcarts, bartering for everything from hats to honey-bread. From her vantage point on Ajax, Hazel saw a water-seller struggling under the weight of his tanks; a printer with ink-stained fingers hawking news pamphlets; two noblemen in frock coats and wigs walking arm in arm out of a haberdashery, and a beggar child creeping behind them with her eyes fixed on their pockets.

'Stop fidgeting, girl,' Titus snapped as Hazel wriggled behind him. 'Keep still!'

'I want to see what's *happening*.'

'Oh, come here.' Titus lifted her up and sat her in front of him. 'Happy now?'

Hazel grinned and nodded.

'Well, I'm not,' Bramley said from behind her ear. 'This

19

place is far too noisy. And what if I fall? I'll be trampled into mush under all those feet.'

A butcher emerged from his shop and hurled a bucket of offal into the gutter. Mangy dogs and even mangier children dived in to fight over the scraps.

'Watch it, idiot!' Titus shouted.

The butcher made a gesture that Hazel supposed was extremely rude and stomped back inside.

'When was the last time you were in London?' she asked.

'About a thousand years ago,' Titus replied. 'The College of Witch Finders was based in Baynards Castle, although I spent most of my time on the road – I never did like staying in one place for too long.'

'Where do you think they'll be keeping Murrell?' Bramley said.

'They probably have him in the Tower of London, but I know a place where we can find out for sure.'

'You're taking us to a tavern, aren't you?' Hazel said, digging her elbow into Titus's ribs.

'I am, and for three good reasons. One, we need a discreet place to stay. Two, information. If you want to know *anything*, a tavern is the best place to ask. And three—'

'So you can get drunk,' Bramley said.

'Now listen, girl and her rat,' Titus growled. 'We've been travelling for nearly a month. My arse is aching, my spirits are low, and this fool's errand is likely to be the death of me. So, yes, I'm bloody well going to have a drink.'

'I think it's best we don't argue about this,' Bramley

whispered. Hazel was inclined to agree.

Titus steered Ajax out of the crowd and down a quiet side street. Here, the eaves of the houses on either side were so close together they had to ride down the middle to avoid hitting their heads. The clamour of the crowd receded, the smell of refuse grew.

Hazel's initial excitement at entering the city was slowly replaced by an unnerving claustrophobia. There were too many people, too many soldiers, too many walls and gates . . .

Bramley stroked her neck with his tail as they made their slow, crooked way deeper into Southwark's backstreet maze – an airless, decaying place where the people they passed were dirty and thin and watched them through narrowed eyes.

'They don't like strangers around here,' Titus said.

'And we're already a pretty strange bunch,' Bramley said.

At last they emerged into a sunlit courtyard. On the far side was a thatched tavern with a timber balcony and a sign in the shape of a rearing horse.

'I'm glad to find my legs still work,' Titus said as he dismounted and stretched enough to make his joints crack.

A grubby boy with strands of straw in his hair emerged from a stable. 'Staying at the Bannered Mare, mister?' he asked.

'We are.' Titus flipped him a coin. 'This is my horse, Ajax. He needs fresh oats and a brush down.'

The boy nodded and took the reins as Hazel slid off the

saddle and joined Titus by the door.

He looked down at her. 'Rat-catchers, right?'

'Right. And I'm Elizabeth, *right?*'

Titus grunted and led the way into a low-ceilinged barroom with a scattering of early afternoon patrons. Hazel was pleased to find it cool and filled with a not unpleasant smell of tobacco and ale.

There was no one serving at the bar so Titus turned to a ferocious-looking woman sloshing her mop over the floor. 'Excuse me, madam . . . ?'

'Mr *Treacher!*' she bellowed without looking up.

A cheerful voice echoed from a back room. 'Coming, my little dove!'

Titus raised an eyebrow at Hazel, and she hid a smile behind her hand.

A barrel-shaped man with a nose the colour of claret appeared behind the bar. 'There she is,' he said. 'The woman I married. Red-faced and furious, just the way I like her.'

'A fine specimen of the fairer sex,' Titus remarked.

'Aye, that she is.' Mr Treacher gave his wife an adoring look as she hurled the bucket of dirty mop water out of the front door, narrowly missing a passing gang of dockworkers.

'My name is Mr Arthur Lowe,' Titus said, 'and I'll have a pint of your best. And this is my daughter, Lizzie. She'll have a small beer.'

'I'd prefer water,' Hazel said, hopping up on to a stool.

'Water?' Treacher laughed, handing Titus his drink. 'I don't recommend that, Lizzie.'

'Why not?'

Titus stared into his mug as if it contained the meaning of life and then took a long swallow. 'London water's not safe to drink,' he said, wiping the froth from his moustache. 'Small beer for you.'

'All right. But I don't want a small one. I'll have a normal-sized one, please.'

'Small doesn't mean small as in *small*,' Treacher said. 'Small beer is watered-down ale you can drink without getting drunk.'

'No fun at all,' Titus said. 'But perfect for little girls.'

'Very well then, I'll have a large small beer.'

'Right you are,' Treacher said.

'I don't suppose *I* get a drink?' Bramley whispered in Hazel's ear.

'Do you have any rooms, Mr Treacher?' Titus said.

'We do,' he replied, passing Hazel a mug. 'Plenty, actually. Business is slow in the Bannered Mare, I'm afraid.'

'Why's that?' Hazel asked.

'There's been a plague outbreak hereabouts.'

'The soldier at the gates told us it was caused by the witch prisoners held by the Order,' Hazel said. She took an experimental swallow of beer and found that it warmed her insides in a surprisingly pleasant way.

'Mm, well, I don't know about that,' Treacher said. 'I'm old enough to remember when witches weren't blamed for every ill that blew in on the wind. Mrs Treacher's grandmother – God rest her –had a touch of magic about her and she never did anyone any harm.' He sighed. 'Times have changed, and not for the better.'

'Agreed.' Titus lowered his voice. 'We've also heard that the Witch Hunters have captured Nicolas Murrell.'

Treacher nodded darkly. 'Aye. Brought him in a few weeks ago. I heard he was trying to summon a demon by sacrificing children . . .' He cast a glance at Hazel and trailed off. 'I don't know if it's true or not, but plenty of folks are willing to believe it.'

'Keeping him in the Tower, are they?' Titus said.

Treacher shook his head. 'A prisoner as important as him will be locked up on Cromwell Island.'

'What's Cromwell Island?' Hazel asked.

Treacher leaned closer. 'It's the Witch Hunters' new prison. They only finished it last year. Built it right in the middle of the Thames.' He shuddered. 'Terrible place. Escape-proof.'

'An escape-proof island?' Bramley squeaked. 'That doesn't sound too hopeful.'

'There's a view of it from London Bridge, if you're curious,' Treacher continued. 'Right, I'll get your rooms made up. You'd like some food in the meantime?'

Hazel's stomach rumbled. 'Yes, please.'

'And another ale,' Titus said, tapping his mug.

'Right you are.'

Hazel and Titus found a quiet table in an adjoining room and sat down.

'I told you we'd get news at an inn,' Titus said.

'I don't like what the landlord said about that island,' Bramley said, climbing into Hazel's lap. 'If it's as impregnable as he says . . .'

Hazel tapped him on the nose. 'Let's wait until we've seen it before we start panicking.'

Mr Treacher brought over more ale and a board laden with bread and butter, cheese, and thick slices of ham. 'Here you go. Let me know if you need anything else.'

'There's nothing there for me,' Bramley whined.

'I thought rats liked cheese,' Titus said, tearing into the bread.

Hazel saw Bramley bristle, so she hastily cut off a slice of her pear and put it on her lap for him to nibble on. They ate in silence until Titus leaned back in his chair and regarded Hazel from under his furrowed brow.

'Well?' she said, picking through the remains of the ham. 'Spit it out.'

'I want you to be prepared.'

'Prepared for what?'

'Failure. If my long and eventful life has taught me anything, it's that things don't often end happily.' He looked down, lost in thought. 'Hell, sometimes things don't end at all, they just get worse.'

Hazel looked at the Witch Finder's craggy face and wondered, not for the first time, what hardships he'd endured over the years. 'Maybe you're right,' she said. 'But that's not going to stop me trying.'

'I admire your determination, but if a thing's impossible,

it's impossible, and you just have to let it go, right?'

Hazel folded her arms. 'Wrong.'

'Let's just take a look at this island, shall we?' Bramley said. 'Then we can talk about what to do next.'

Titus drained the last of his ale. 'Well don't say I didn't warn you, slop-sprite.'

They were about to leave when a dirty-haired girl in a ragged dress sidled up to their table and held out her hand. 'Spare a coin for a plague orphan?'

Titus turned his sternest glare on to her. 'Do I look like I'm made of money?'

Hazel smiled and slid the remains of the food across the table. 'Here – have this.'

'Not the pear!' Bramley hissed at Hazel. 'Oh, too late,' he added dejectedly, as the girl hastily wrapped everything up in a grubby handkerchief.

'How old are you?' Titus asked.

'Eight and a half,' the girl replied.

'Eight and a half?' he boomed. 'You look about six. I've seen more meat on a dirty fork.'

Hazel kicked him under the table.

'Oh, very well,' he said, handing over a couple of coins. 'Now, be off with you.'

The girl gave a little bow and scampered away.

'Too soft-hearted, that's my trouble,' Titus grumbled.

Hazel snorted. 'Come on, let's take a look at this island.'

4
FLASK AND STUBB'S

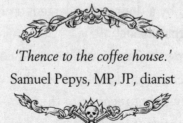

'Thence to the coffee house.'
Samuel Pepys, MP, JP, diarist

T ired as they were from their journey into Southwark, Hazel and Titus roused themselves and headed back out into the sultry, mid-afternoon sun. Bramley took residence behind Hazel's ear and began to clean his whiskers of pear juice.

'You'd better memorize the route, Hazel,' Titus said. 'If we lose each other you'll need to find your way back here. Believe me, you don't want to get lost in Southwark.'

'Don't worry about me. I have an excellent sense of direction.'

'Since when?' Bramley said.

'Since always.'

Titus stopped in the middle of the courtyard. 'Prove it. Take us back to Southwark High Road.'

'Fine.' Hazel chose the alley that she was *pretty* certain they had arrived down. 'It's this way.'

The heat trapped under the eaves prickled her skin with sweat and made her dress stick to her back. Lanes branched

27

off in both directions, narrower still and quickly kinking out of sight.

She stopped by a door with a large red cross painted on it. 'What does that mean?'

'It's a warning to stay away,' Titus replied. 'Some poor wretch in there has got the plague, so they've been locked inside until they either recover, or die.'

'But that's *terrible*,' Hazel said.

'It's the law – a precaution to stop the disease from spreading.'

'Doesn't anyone help them?' Bramley asked.

'Friends or neighbours might bring food.' Titus shrugged. 'But beyond that, no.'

'Ma would be able to do something,' Hazel said hotly. 'She knows all sorts of healing spells. Don't men like Hopkins realize that Wielders could make this city a better place?'

Titus laid his hand on her shoulder in a rare display of affection. 'Hazel, you need to learn that men like Hopkins would hate witches even if they could cure all the ills in the world.'

'But *why?*'

'Because you're women in a world ruled jealously by men, and you possess power beyond their understanding and control. That power – and I'm not just talking about your magic – frightens them to their core.'

Hazel frowned. 'What power are you talking about?'

'The power to see the wrongs in this world and the desire

to do something about it,' Titus said. 'Your mother had it, I had it, and in a way so did Murrell.' His gaze focused on something far away. 'That's why we fought in the Witch War all those years ago, and that's why the rebels in the North are carrying on that fight.'

'Come on, time's pressing,' Bramley chided.

By keeping to the upward slope and then following the noise of the crowd, Hazel finally led them on to Southwark High Road. 'There – I did it!'

'Not bad,' Titus said with a grudging nod of respect. 'We'll make a Londoner of you yet.'

The market was in full swing, so Hazel stuck close to Titus as fishmongers, butchers, and fruit, veg and flower sellers all cried their wares at the top of their lungs; the riot of delicious smells was a vast relief after the squalor of the backstreets.

'This is intolerable,' Bramley squeaked as a passing candle seller nearly knocked him from Hazel's shoulder.

'Look ahead,' Titus said. 'That's the entrance to London Bridge.'

Hazel stood on tiptoes and saw a turreted stone gatehouse spanning the street. Red banners emblazoned with the crossed-hammer sign of the Order hung from the ramparts. As they got closer Titus pointed up at a row of decaying heads on spikes. 'Thieves, traitors and murderers,' he said with a wicked grin. 'But no witches – they tend to burn your type.'

'What a relief,' Hazel said. 'I hate heights.'

The entrance to the bridge was choked with traffic, but at least this time there were no guards to slow things down.

'Stick close,' Titus said, 'and don't get lost.'

Hazel followed the old Witch Finder through the gatehouse and out on to a narrow street lined with shops, taverns and chophouses. She caught a whiff of sewage and a glimpse of grey water between some buildings before the crowd pushed her on.

'We need a view of the Island,' she said. 'A place to get a really good look.'

Titus stopped outside a tavern. 'How about here? There's bound to be a window overlooking the river, and I could do with another drink.'

Voices drifted from a whitewash-and-timber building next door. A sign hanging over the eave read 'Flask and Stubb's Coffee House'.

'Ooh, coffee!' Hazel said, tugging a reluctant Titus through the door. 'I hear it sharpens the mind wonderfully.'

'Oh, all right . . .'

Inside was an oak-panelled room crammed from serving bar to bay windows with finely dressed, periwigged men drinking out of china cups. Red-faced serving girls poured coffee from an enormous copper tureen hanging over a fire – it smelt rich and reviving.

'These syrup-of-soot houses are springing up everywhere,' Titus grumbled.

'There's a free table by the window,' Bramley said. 'Quick, before someone takes it.'

A couple of merchants in velvet coats were already homing in, so Hazel wormed her way in front of them, smiling sweetly as she slid into the seat. One merchant opened his mouth to protest but thought better of it when Titus loomed up behind him.

'Our table, I believe,' he rumbled. The merchants retreated.

Hazel, Titus and Bramley stared out of the window overlooking the Thames, and for a few moments sat in stunned silence.

A round tower of smooth black stone rose up from the middle of the river. Devoid of architectural features – no windows, no balconies, no buttresses – it tapered up to a flat roof lined with crenellated battlements, looking for all the world like a giant chess piece.

'So *that's* Cromwell Island,' Hazel said.

'God's bones,' Titus groaned.

'That's not a prison, it's a fortress,' Bramley said. 'What hope do we have of getting in there?'

'This is worse than we thought.' Titus gestured to a serving girl to bring some coffee.

'There must be a way for us to get inside,' Hazel said. 'There *must.*'

Titus took a small brass telescope from his pocket, extended it with a flick of his wrist and put it to his eye. After a few moments of grim surveillance he said, 'I see a bridge connecting it to the north bank of the river . . . That's the only way in and it's bound to be heavily guarded.'

31

'Perhaps we could take a boat out there and climb up?' Hazel said.

Bramley nipped her ear. 'That's a crazy idea even for you.'

'Well, we have to think of something,' Hazel murmured, feeling the hope she had carefully nurtured drain away. 'We've come so far already . . .'

'All right – for argument's sake, let's say we got inside the Island and found Murrell,' Titus said, putting the telescope away. 'We have to remember that he's been at the mercy of the Witch Hunters for a month now – he might not be in a fit state to help us at all.'

Hazel looked him in the eye. 'Well, I'm going to try anyway.'

'Dammit, girl! He's probably dead already.'

'He's alive. I just know it.'

'No you *don't*.' Titus slapped his hand on the table hard enough to rattle the cutlery. 'You don't know anything, and that's a bad position from which to make a plan.'

A serving girl appeared, set a coffee pot and two cups on the table and then eased her way back into the crowd.

Hazel folded her arms, drawing deep from her bottomless well of determination. 'I'm not giving up. We'll just have to ask around, find out all we can about the Island and plan a way in.'

Bramley and Titus exchanged a worried glance.

'Look,' Hazel said, pointing to a decrepit sailing ship moored at the foot of the Island. 'That must be the prison hulk the soldier was talking about.'

Titus trained his telescope on it. 'An old fighting ship. A carrack, judging by her lines. Mmm, the gun hatches have been sealed shut – the prisoners must be trapped below decks, locked in with the rats.'

The table rocked as he leaned his elbows on it. Cursing, he picked up a news pamphlet and began folding it into a wedge to put under the table leg.

'Wait a moment . . .' Hazel snatched it from him. 'Look at this, at the bottom of the page.'

Titus squinted and read out loud: '*Vacancy for a Junior Apprentice in the Order of Witch Hunters. Applicants report to the Tower of London at ten o'clock, 12th July.*' He looked up. 'So?'

Hazel grinned, suppressing a warm wash of magic. 'If the Witch Hunters are looking for recruits, I should heed their call!'

'*What?*' Titus and Bramley said in unison.

'This is my way into Cromwell Island,' Hazel said, brandishing the pamphlet. '*This is my way to Nicolas Murrell.*'

5
A SIMPLE PLAN

'**Y**ou said yourself that Murrell's on borrowed time,' Hazel continued before Bramley or Titus had time to speak. 'I must get to him soon or we've no hope of rescuing Ma. And this way means there's no need for a break-in that's bound to fail. Don't you see?'

'The principle of your plan does not elude me, and neither does its sheer recklessness,' Titus said. 'And there's something else you haven't considered.'

'And what's that?'

'The Order only takes boys, and you *happen* to be a girl.'

'He's right, Hazel,' Bramley said, nervously flicking his tail. 'And lest we forget, you're also a Wielder.'

'I can hide my magic. I do it all the time.'

'Do you? Really?' Titus said. 'It gets the better of you some-times. I saw it just now – a little flash of light like a halo.' He jerked his thumb towards the Tower. 'If those men find out you're a Wielder, they won't let you off by just killing you. Oh no. They have devices, techniques, *administrations* . . .'

'I'll control it, I promise,' Hazel said. 'What else can I say? I'm doing it. I have to. For Ma.'

'You'll be unprepared and alone, walking into the middle of a pack of wolves.'

'Ma would do the same for me.' Hazel shrugged. 'And I think you would too, old man.'

Titus shook his head. 'That's not the point . . .'

'And anyway, I'll not be alone.' Hazel pointed to where Bramley perched on her shoulder. 'Bram'll be with me.'

Titus shot him a look. 'Will you?'

Bramley's whiskers drooped. 'A familiar never abandons his witch.'

'Well?' Hazel said, keeping her eyes fixed on Titus. 'Will you help me?'

'Stubborn, *stubborn* witch . . .' Titus stared down at his gnarled hands.

Hazel waited. She knew Titus well by now, and saw the worry in every line in his face. He cared about her, wanted to protect her, and yet here she was asking him to help her walk into terrible danger. Guilt swirled in her stomach. She pushed it away.

'You're determined to go through with this, aren't you?' Titus eventually said.

Hazel nodded.

'And without my help you'll probably get caught and killed within five minutes.'

She nodded again.

Titus closed his eyes and let out a long sigh. 'You'll need

boys' clothes, and a boy's name.'

'Thank you.' Hazel took his hand and gave it a squeeze. 'How about William? I like William.'

'And a family history and plausible reasons for joining the Order,' Titus continued. 'The Witch Hunters will ask you questions and you'll have to be able to answer convincingly.' He jabbed a finger at the date on the flyer. 'And you've only got until ten o'clock tomorrow to prepare. So, *William*, what's your story?'

'How about I'm the son of a rat-catcher, but the business is in ruins because my father's a drunkard?' She smiled. 'That shouldn't be too hard to imagine.'

Titus gave her a stern look. 'You need to take this seriously, Hazel. One false move, one mistake, and they'll get you.'

'I know,' she sighed, 'but if I don't laugh about it I'll be too scared to go.'

Titus drained his coffee and put some coins on the table. 'I'll see to the clothes. You go back to the inn, get some rest, and get your story straight.'

'I'll help her practise,' Bramley said.

'Good idea. Can you find your way back on your own?'

'You saw how well I did before,' Hazel said.

Titus grunted. 'Don't speak to anyone. London is full of informants, so treat everyone like an enemy.'

'I'll be fine,' she said, rolling her eyes. 'Stop worrying.'

'Oh, of course – stop worrying. Easy. I'll stop breathing too while I'm at it, shall I?'

Hazel smiled and patted him on the arm – her mother used to say the same thing.

The oppressive heat of the day had lifted by the time Hazel emerged from the gatehouse on to Southwark High Road, and she was relieved to find that the crowds had thinned out.

Pretending to be a boy would be a challenge – David was the only one she'd ever met properly, and he was a few years older than her. *Perhaps I should imagine myself as a young Titus*, she thought, but then dismissed the idea because she just couldn't picture him as anything other than an old man.

Pleased that her sense of direction had not deserted her, she found her way back to the Bannered Mare despite Bramley's attempts to help: 'Left here. Or is it right? Perhaps we should have taken that turn by the fish stall . . .'

'There you are, Lizzie!' Mr Treacher waved at her from behind the bar. 'Shall I show you to your room? It's all ready.'

'Yes, please,' she said with a nod.

'Follow me then, my tulip,' he said. 'I've put you at the back where it's quiet. You on your own?'

'Yes. Father's out looking for customers.'

'He can sort this place out if he likes. Mrs T's been on at me about the cellar.'

'You'll have to head him off at the pass on *that*,' Bramley whispered. 'Titus doesn't know the first thing about catching rats.'

'I think he's trying to get work in the City,' Hazel said.

'Well, I suppose the pay's better over the river.' Treacher led her up a rambling set of stairs. 'Ah, hello, my dove!'

Mrs Treacher was standing on the landing with brushes and cloths tucked under her arms; her eyes lingered on Hazel for an uncomfortably long time before she stomped back towards the bar.

'Don't mind Mrs T,' Treacher said, ushering Hazel through a door. 'Here we are. This is your room, and your father's is next door.'

The room was small and cosy, with a washstand in the corner and an inviting bed piled high with pillows.

'We're right over the water here.' Treacher handed her a key. 'There's a back door at the end of the corridor leading to the balcony. You can get down to the street from there if you want to avoid the barroom crowd.'

'Thank you, Mr Treacher, you've been most helpful.'

'Well, it's nice for Mrs T and me to have a girl around the place.' Treacher smiled. 'I'd best get back to work. I'll send some supper up for you later.'

As soon as the door closed Bramley jumped on to the bed and rolled around, kicking his legs in the air. 'Oh, that feels good. I've been cooped up in your hair for ages.'

'I'm afraid you'll be spending a lot more time in there. We can't let the Witch Hunters see you.' Hazel lay back on the bed and stretched out her arms. 'Do you think our plan will work?'

'Well, let me see . . . Will we manage to infiltrate the

Witch Hunters' lair, convince Murrell to help you *despite* the fact it was your meddling that got him arrested, then travel into the Underworld to rescue your Ma from Baal the demon prince? Do you really want me to answer that?'

'Perhaps not,' Hazel sighed. 'But we can improve our chances by preparing for tomorrow.'

Bramley settled down on a pillow. 'All right. I'll be the Witch Hunter questioning you. You be you being a boy called William. Ready?'

'Yes. Go!'

For the next two hours Bramley fired question after question at Hazel: 'Where were you born? . . . What is your mother's maiden name? . . . Do you have any brothers or sisters?' Next he coached her on how to walk more like a boy: 'Try longer strides, and add a touch of swagger . . . No, no, no, that's a *lollop* . . .'

By the time the sun had set, Hazel felt frazzled, but she had memorized a fictional family history, and felt more confident that she could pass as a boy.

'It's getting late,' she said, using a flare of magic to light the candles. 'Where's Titus got to?'

'Who knows?' Bramley yawned. 'Probably drunk in a gutter.'

Hazel picked him up. 'Come on, let's get some air.'

6
A BREATH OF AIR

Using the key Treacher had given her, Hazel unlocked the back door and stepped outside on to the balcony. It was muggy, with only the faintest breath of wind coming from the river.

'Tide's out,' she said. 'Just look at all that mud.'

'I know, I can smell it,' Bramley huffed. '"Let's get some air," she says. Huh. Brilliant idea.'

Hazel put up her hood and descended the stairs on to a rambling network of jetties; it was a long drop to the riverbed. The far bank glimmered with lights, and distant shouts and laughter drifted over the bubbling mudflats – but in Southwark there was not a single soul to be seen. *Where is everyone?* Hazel wondered, making her way down an alley squeezed between the Bannered Mare and a row of houses.

'It's too quiet,' Bramley said. 'I don't like it.'

'You don't like noise, you don't like quiet. What *do* you like?'

'A warm nest and a full stomach, neither of which I have.'

Hazel stopped at a junction. Ahead was the Bannered Mare's courtyard. A few men stood by the stables, talking in the glow of a lantern. To the right another alley led deeper into the warren of buildings. She took it, walking slowly through the deserted darkness.

'Why are we going down here?' Bramley said.

'I need to learn my way around and—'

A scream echoed from a passage ahead. Hazel froze. 'What was that?'

Bramley nearly fell off her shoulder in fright. 'I think it's time for us to go back to the inn now,' he squeaked.

'But someone might be in trouble.' Hazel sidled forward and pressed herself against a wall. 'I think it came from down here . . .'

'Careful!' Bramley whispered.

Hazel peeked round the corner and saw a ragged girl with a mass of filthy hair lying prostrate about ten paces down the passage. Her breath came in shallow gasps, and her mouth was open as if she was still screaming.

Hazel wanted to rush over to see if she was hurt, but instinct held her back. Something had caused the girl to collapse in a dead faint, and whatever it was could still be nearby.

'Bram?' she said. 'Can you smell that?'

'Yes, I can. What is that – milk?'

Hazel wrinkled her nose. '*Sour* milk. But where's it . . . ?'

A figure emerged from behind a stack of barrels halfway

down the passage. It wore a floor-length robe of leather and a hat with a brim wide enough to veil its face in shadow. Bent double, shoulders hunched, it crept silently towards the girl with a malevolent intent that made Hazel's blood run cold.

'What is that thing?' Bramley whispered.

The figure circled the girl like a vulture deliberating which part of its prey to peck first. Hypnotized with horror, Hazel watched as it slowly peeled off one of its gloves and reached down with long white fingers.

Gathering a crackling ball of magic around her fist, Hazel stepped out into the mouth of the passage. 'Leave her alone!' she cried, turning side-on in readiness to wield.

The figure swivelled towards her. Hazel's firelight illuminated a long beak-like nose and two flat, unblinking eyes. Before she could decide if what she was seeing was even human, it unbent to its full, obscene height. Up it rose, slender, menacing, taller than Titus, taller than any man she'd ever laid eyes on.

'Witch!' it hissed, unfurling one of its long fingers towards her.

Terror crawled up Hazel's spine and tried to make her run, but she stood where she was, drawing strength from the fire that crackled around her fingers. She narrowed her eyes and made her voice as strong as she could.

'That's right, I'm a witch – a *Fire* Witch – so leave her alone *before I burn you up.*'

The figure stayed quite still for what seemed like an

age and then seeped silently back into the shadows, taking the smell of sour milk with it. A whisper drifted from the darkness – 'Another time' – and then it was gone.

'What *was* that thing?' Bramley said, quivering from nose to tail.

'I don't know,' Hazel said, hurrying down the passage. 'But we need to get this poor girl out of here before it comes back.' She pushed the hair away from the girl's face and let out a cry of horror. 'Oh, Bram, *look*. It's the beggar girl we met this afternoon.'

The girl was only skin and bone but Hazel was panting by the time she'd carried her up the steps and through the back door of the tavern.

'Mr Treacher,' she called. 'I need help, quickly!'

Mrs Treacher emerged from a room at the end of the corridor. 'What's all this racket . . . ?' The duster dropped from her hand when she saw the girl in Hazel's arms. 'Oh goodness, what's happened?'

'I found her in a passage nearby.' Hazel shouldered her bedroom door open. 'Can you help me?'

'Of course. Oh, the poor little thing . . .'

Together they lay the girl down on the bed and covered her with blankets.

'What happened to her?' Mrs Treacher said, clasping the girl's hand.

'She was attacked by . . . something. What it was, I don't know.'

43

The colour drained from Mrs Treacher's face. 'I think I'd better get my husband,' she said, and hurried from the room.

'She's still not come round,' Bramley said, emerging on to Hazel's shoulder and peering at the girl. 'Give her a shake.'

'She's been frightened nearly to death,' Hazel murmured, noting that under the layers of grime the girl's hair was a rich red colour similar to her own.

'You saw how tall it was? And that face . . . It wasn't human, surely?'

Hurried footsteps approached the door, and Bramley only just managed to dive back into Hazel's hair before both Treachers burst into the room.

'. . . and Lizzie said she found her lying right near where the others were found,' Mrs Treacher was saying to her frowning husband.

'Others?' Bramley whispered. 'What others?'

'Oh dear, oh dear, what a terrible to-do,' Mr Treacher said, rubbing his hands fretfully on his apron. 'Lizzie, can you tell us what happened?'

As Mrs Treacher gently washed the girl's face and hands, Hazel recounted the events, being careful to leave out all mention of her magic.

'The figure crept away when I shouted at it, then I picked the girl up and carried her here as quickly as I could.'

Mr Treacher puffed out his cheeks. 'That was brave of you. Very brave. You probably saved her life.'

'Mrs Treacher,' Hazel said. 'You mentioned there were

"others". What did you mean?'

Wife and husband shared a look and then Mrs Treacher, still running a cloth over the girl's forehead said quietly, 'There have been deaths in Southwark, all children, their bodies found in alleys . . . No one knows how they died. Most people are too scared to go out at night.'

'We'll spread the word tomorrow about this fiend who stalks our streets,' Mr Treacher added.

Hazel was about to question them further when the door opened and Titus walked in with a bundle under his arm. He took in the scene, face unreadable. 'So, Lizzie, what have you been up to now?'

Agreeing without question to look after the girl, the Treachers carried her to a spare room with such care that Hazel's heart burst with warmth towards them.

After their footsteps had disappeared Titus leaned back on the windowsill and folded his arms. 'Can't leave you alone for five minutes, can I? You'd better tell me what happened.'

Hazel sat on the bed with Bramley on her knee and related everything that had happened since they'd parted. The old Witch Hunter listened carefully, eyes bright under his craggy brow.

'A beak, no mouth, and strange, round eyes,' he murmured. 'Could it have been a mask?'

'Perhaps,' Hazel said. 'The passage was dark and it all happened so quickly.'

'What about you, Master Mouse? What do you remember?'

Bramley's whiskers twitched. 'I remember smelling sour milk just before I saw it. Horrible.'

Titus tugged on his beard. 'And the Treachers said there have been other deaths that might be related to this?'

Hazel nodded. 'Yes, so I think we should go out and look . . .'

Titus held up his hand. 'Stop right there, girl. You've got enough on your plate without taking this thorny problem on as well. Leave it be.'

'But—'

'No, Hazel. Just for once will you listen to what I say? I'll investigate your mysterious skulker myself, all right? It'll give me something to do while you're away.'

Bramley tugged her ear. 'He's right. You need to rest, get ready for tomorrow.'

'Oh all right, but be careful, old man,' Hazel said. 'Whatever that thing is, it's big.'

'I can look after myself, thank you.' Titus tapped the bundle at his feet. 'There's boys' clothes in there, and scissors to cut your hair.'

Bramley looked aghast. 'But her hair – that's where I *live*.'

'I'll make sure there's enough left for you to nest in,' Hazel said, running her finger down his back.

'And make sure the Treachers don't see you dressed as a boy – that would throw up far too many questions,' Titus

46

added. 'Did you practise your story for the Witch Hunters? Got it all straight?'

Hazel picked up the bundle and began to undo it. 'Yes, and Bramley can whisper in my ear if I forget anything.'

'All good, all good . . .' Titus muttered. 'Now get a decent night's sleep.'

'I will. Thanks, Titus.' Hazel gave him a grateful smile. 'Wish me luck for tomorrow.'

'Luck be damned,' he growled. 'Use your wits if you want to survive.'

After cutting her hair to just above the shoulders – a task she found surprisingly distressing – Hazel crawled into bed and stared up into the darkness. Bramley lay on the pillow next to her, snoring gently with his mouth open.

Tomorrow she would be facing down men who would kill her if they knew what she was. She had her story off by heart, the skills to lie and just enough mastery over her magic to keep it hidden, but still her heart thumped like a drum in her chest.

It was this *waiting*. It gave her too much time to think, to worry about Bramley, her mother, even Titus.

I just want to get on with it, she thought, closing her eyes. *And get it over with*.

Sleep took her sooner than expected. It had, after all, been a long and eventful day.

7
THE WHITE TOWER

When Hazel woke the next morning it took her a few moments to recall where she was. And then, with a rush of adrenalin, she remembered.

Today I stick my head in the dragon's mouth. I hope it doesn't bite.

She judged from the sun's position that it was about seven o'clock. The selection was at ten so she had three hours to get to the Tower of London. She put on the clothes Titus had bought for her – black woollen breeches, linen shirt and a short, buttoned jacket – and muttered 'My name is William Lowe, I come from Putney, and I'm the son of a rat-catcher' over and over again.

'Not bad,' Bramley yawned from the pillow. 'Being a boy suits you.'

'And the hair? Is it all right?'

Bramley cocked his head. 'Yes, I think so.'

'Should I cut more off?'

'No!' Bramley squeaked. 'You've got to leave me somewhere to hide.'

Hazel jammed a baggy cloth cap over her head. 'There. The disguise is complete.'

'Wait a minute!' Bramley said, looking around in mock surprise. 'Where did Hazel go? Hazel, where *are* you?'

'Ha, ha. Very funny.' She whisked him up and deposited him on her shoulder. 'Let's wake the grouch.'

There was no answer when she knocked on Titus's door, so she poked her head inside. He was asleep, still fully dressed on top of the bedcovers.

'He's still got his boots on,' Bramley said disgustedly.

Hazel closed the door and headed outside the back way.

'Aren't you going to say goodbye?' Bramley asked.

'No. Let him sleep. He'll only want to come with me, and what would be the point of that? We'll have to leave him behind when we get to the Tower anyway.'

'And you hate goodbyes.'

'I do. I really do.'

Hazel hurried on to Southwark High Road and across London Bridge. The streets were busy with morning trade and people hurrying to work, but as she darted her way through the crowd with Bramley behind her ear she found the going easier than it had been the day before.

I'm getting used to the heat, bustle and noise, she thought as she turned down a lane skirting the riverbank eastwards towards the Tower. *But I would give anything to be back in the Glade again with Ma.*

'I wonder how the girl is this morning,' Bramley said, breaking her train of thought. 'I hope she wakes up.'

'Me too. Poor thing. It's just as well we were there last night, or who knows what would have happened.'

'Yes, we were very brave, weren't we?'

'Yes, Bram. You especially.'

Nerves stole Hazel's appetite but she knew she had to eat to keep her thoughts lucid, so she bought a bread roll filled with salted pork and ate it as she walked.

She descended some steps on to a street with a view of the Thames and a seemingly endless line of moored ships – a blessed relief after the built-up confines of London Bridge. Ahead rose the pale stone pile of the Tower of London, its layers of fortifications and the White Tower itself glaring in the sun.

Bramley tugged her ear. 'There are some boys over there by that gate – perhaps they're waiting for the selection too.'

Gathering her courage, Hazel hurried across the pavement and joined them. A few of the older boys looked her up and down, but appeared to decide she wasn't much of a threat.

'This lot seem to think you look like a boy,' Bramley whispered. 'Try talking to one of them.'

Hazel sidled over to a small, nervous looking lad standing a little apart from the rest. 'Hello, my name's Will,' she said as gruffly as she could. 'Are you here for the selection?'

'What's *that* voice all of a sudden?' Bramley hissed. 'Stop it – you sound ridiculous.'

Hazel coughed and reverted to her normal tone. 'Sorry about that – got a bit of a cold.'

'I'm Anthony,' the boy replied. 'Yes, I'm here for the selection.' He was shorter than Hazel, and thin beneath his ragged clothes.

Before she could reply one of the gate-tower doors creaked open. 'Someone's coming,' one of the boys whispered as a tall, middle-aged man wearing a fur-lined cloak over his Witch Hunter uniform strode towards them. Two guards followed, grinning through their helmet visors.

'Clear the way, you beggars and scoundrels,' the Witch Hunter said. 'Go on, be off with you, you raggedy lot.'

The boys shuffled nervously and some took a few paces backwards. Hazel stood her ground, sensing that this was some sort of test.

'Guards!' the Witch Hunter said. 'See 'em off or spike 'em with your swords, I don't care which.'

'No one respects fear, so don't show any,' Bramley whispered as the guards advanced. 'And this old windbag is all bluster.'

The boys backed further away, leaving Hazel exposed with Anthony standing behind her. The Witch Hunter glared, but she refused to wither.

'I'm not a beggar,' she said, holding out the flyer. 'I'm here for the selection. I want to work for the Order.'

Anthony held up his hand. 'Me too.'

The Witch Hunter regarded Hazel for a moment. 'Very

well,' he said, and marched back towards the gate, his cloak sweeping the ground.

Hazel and the rest followed him through the gate and out on to a walkway. On the left rose a huge stone wall encircling the White Tower, and on the right a wide embankment sloped down to the river. Ahead was a heavily guarded bridge spanning the river to Cromwell Island.

I'm in, Hazel thought, feeling a wobble in her legs. *But will I make it out?*

The Witch Hunter stopped by an archway, through which Hazel caught a glimpse of a lawn and a portion of the White Tower's massive foundation stones.

'I am Sir Edward Grimstone,' he said, resting his hand on an ornately carved pistol holstered by his side. 'It's my job to decide if any of you are fit to work for the Order. My first impression is that none of you are, but as a professional I am bound to go through the motions.'

One boy waved his hand. 'Sir Grimestone—'

'It's *Grimstone*, idiot!'

The boy cringed. 'Sorry, Sir Grimstone . . . but will we get to meet *him?*'

'Him?' Grimstone's mouth curved into a smile. 'By "him" I suppose you mean General Hopkins? You will meet him, but only if you make it through the selection process. Follow me.'

He led them through the archway into the grassy courtyard. The White Tower loomed up over them, crossed-hammer pennants fluttering from the heights. A pavilion stood against a wall, and inside six stern men sat behind desks. Hazel didn't like the look of them one bit.

'Those men are interrogators,' Grimstone said. 'They have interrupted their normal duties on Cromwell Island to assist me with this selection. They are going to subject each of you to a thorough examination to find out if you are fit in mind, body and spirit to serve the Order.'

'I hope it's not *too* thorough,' Bramley squeaked, burrowing deeper into Hazel's hair.

Perhaps I should have left Bram behind, Hazel thought. *For his sake as well as mine.*

'Right,' Grimstone said. 'Six of you – in you go.'

No one moved.

Grimstone jabbed Hazel in the back. 'Go on then, if you're so eager to prove yourself.'

'This is it,' Bramley whispered. 'Do it just like we practised.'

Hazel stood up straight and marched up to the nearest desk.

8
SELECTION

Hazel stood at attention in front of the interrogator's desk with her hands clasped behind her back.

I need to appear smart and obedient, she thought. *I reckon that's what the Order wants from its apprentices.*

'Name?' the interrogator said without even looking up from his ledger.

'William Lowe,' Hazel said.

'William Lowe, *sir*.'

'Oh, sorry . . . er, sir . . .'

'Age?'

'Eleven and a half, sir.'

'And where are you from?'

'Putney, sir.'

'Father's occupation?'

'He's partnered in a business, sir. Saxondale and Lowe's, Rat-Catchers.'

The interrogator looked up at her with rheumy eyes. 'Bit small, aren't you?'

54

'I'm stronger than I look,' Hazel replied, standing as straight as she could.

'Physically unimpressive . . .' His quill crawled laboriously across the page.

'But very keen,' Hazel added, already feeling that things were not going her way.

'I'll be the judge of that.' He stood up. 'Take your jacket off and raise your arms over your head.'

Hazel did as she was told, feeling Bramley scramble deeper into her hair. *Please don't find him*, she thought as the interrogator, who smelt unpleasantly of garlic, felt under her arms and scrutinized behind her ears.

'No sign of plague,' he said. 'Stick out your tongue . . . Mmm . . . Well you seem in reasonable health.' He sat back down and wrote another line across the page. 'Now tell me, what is your dominant humour?'

Hazel looked blankly at him. 'My dominant what?'

'Humour, boy, humour.' His inky quill hovered. 'I need it for my ledger.'

'What's he on about?' Bramley whispered.

'Are you sanguine, choleric, melancholic or phlegmatic? Well? Which is it? Come on!'

'I'm, er, melon . . . melon . . . I'm a melon,' Hazel hazarded.

'A *melon*, eh?' The interrogator narrowed his eyes. 'So you don't know about the four humours?'

Hazel deflated, realizing it was useless to bluff. 'No, sir.'

'Ignorant as well as feeble.'

'But I'm very—'

'Keen, yes, you said.' He leaned back and regarded her for a few moments. 'I'm going to ask you some questions. Answer quickly and honestly.'

Hazel nodded, and for the next fifteen minutes endured a barrage of questions about her life, her family, her hopes and dreams, aware that the other candidates were undergoing the same ordeal around her. Some of the questions she had prepared for, some she hadn't, but her practice with Bramley paid off and she answered and improvised with ever increasing confidence.

'One last question, boy.' The interrogator put down his quill. 'Answer carefully. What would you do if you found out your neighbour was a witch?'

The answer seemed obvious: *Denounce her! Turn her over to the Witch Hunters!* Surely that was what he wanted to hear?

But I must convince him I'm the right candidate to join this brutal Order. I've got to stand out from all the others.

The interrogator's expression hardened. 'Well?'

'When I was seven I had a dog called Stripe,' Hazel said, feeling around for a story to string him along with. 'I was taking him for a walk one day when we met an old woman by the roadside. Stripe jumped up at her – he was only being friendly but the woman was furious. She kicked and shouted, her face all twisted with hate.'

Hazel realized she had the interrogator's attention when he put down his quill. Emboldened, she continued to spin her lie.

'I was terrified, so I picked up poor Stripe and ran home. Next morning, he was dead. I told my father what had happened and he said that old woman was a notorious witch, and that most likely she'd laid a curse on poor Stripe and killed him.'

She locked eyes with the interrogator, knowing that what she was about to say went against everything she truly believed. 'That's when I began to *hate* witches, and if I found out my own *mother* was one, I'd kill her on the spot.' Hazel blinked back tears; the ugly, brutal words were like poison on her tongue.

The interrogator looked at her for a long time and then waved her off. 'Go and wait with the others.'

Was it her imagination, or was his voice a little warmer than it had been before?

'I know it couldn't have been easy saying that,' Bramley said. 'But you did the right thing. Now we wait and see.'

Hazel saw Anthony standing despondently outside the pavilion. 'How did you do?' she asked with an encouraging smile.

'I was nervous, and he got impatient. And that made me *more* nervous. I did my best, but . . .'

'I'm sure it wasn't as bad as you think,' Hazel said reassuringly.

The interviews finished. Grimstone and the interrogators gathered together, talking quietly and glancing at the candidates. Hazel bit her lip; she hated waiting.

At last, Grimstone dismissed the assembled men with

a nod and strode up to the applicants. He had a piece of paper in his hand. 'Step forward when I read out your name. Anthony Simpson.'

Anthony looked both surprised and sickened as he edged out of the group.

'Does that mean he's been picked or rejected?' Bramley whispered.

Hazel rather hoped he'd been rejected – Anthony seemed far too nice to work for the Order.

Grimstone looked at her. 'William Lowe.'

Hazel joined Anthony, wondering if she was she in or out.

'Right, the rest of you can go,' Grimstone said. 'William, Anthony, I've chosen you to join the Grand Order of Witch Hunters. Congratulations.'

'You did it,' Bramley squeaked as the failed candidates trudged out of the courtyard. 'Well done!'

Relief burst inside Hazel, and she only just resisted the urge to cry out.

'Thank you, Sir Grimstone,' she said. 'I won't let you down.'

'It's not me you need to worry about,' Grimstone said with a cold smile. 'That would be your new master.'

9
A RISKY DIVULGENCE

'Plague! The Pale Rider! And with him,
behold, the end of the world!'
Apocalyptic Preacher Jeremy Coleman

Titus awoke from a dream, haunted by the memories of long-dead friends and comrades. The room was bright, the sun already riding high. He rolled off the bed and plunged his face into the washbasin, knowing in every aching bone that Hazel had gone to the Tower without him.

Will I lose her too? Just as I've lost everyone else?

A knock at the door broke him out of his thoughts. After pushing the dripping hair from his face and straightening his shirt, Titus opened the door to find Mr Treacher standing outside.

'Ah! Morning, Mr Lowe. I was wondering if you wanted any breakfast?'

Titus stroked his throat. It was dry. He wanted a drink – strong ale to take his mind off Hazel all alone in that den of monsters. 'Can you get me coffee?' he croaked after a brief but considerable internal struggle.

'I can send out the stable boy for a pot,' Treacher said. 'And Lizzie?'

'She's out,' Titus said. 'Meeting a . . . customer.'

'Ah, learning the family trade is she?'

Bitter regret rose in Titus's throat. He thought of David, the boy he'd taken on as his apprentice and then lost to the Order. And now Hazel – gone to them as well.

He beckoned Treacher inside. 'How's the girl?'

'Still dead to the world, poor little creature. Your daughter was very brave last night – she does you credit.'

'Her courage is all her own. Listen, about the attack last night, Lizzie said there have been others?'

Treacher closed the door. 'I'm afraid so. Three children have been found hereabouts in the past few weeks. Found dead, I mean.'

'Do you know who they were?'

'No, the bodies lay unclaimed before being taken to a pauper's grave.' Treacher looked away, blinking furiously. 'They were probably plague orphans with no one to care for them.'

'Is no one investigating this?'

'Course not! The Witch Hunters are the law, and they don't care about a few street urchins.'

Titus stroked his beard, waiting for Treacher to compose himself. 'You seem like a good-hearted fellow, Mr Treacher. May I confide in you?'

'Of course.'

'Before I turned rat-catcher, I was one of the King's own Witch Finders.'

'You don't say?' Treacher's eyes widened.

'I do. Back in the days when Witch Finding was a calling to be proud of, when we sought truth and justice, not the thoughtless persecution against magic-users we see from Hopkins' Hunters.'

Treacher looked nervous; what Titus was saying was treasonous, but after a moment he nodded and said, 'We live in dark times, Mr Lowe. Dark times indeed.'

'I'm glad we see eye to eye.' He held out his hand and Treacher shook it without hesitation. 'Now, I'd like to use my old skills to find out what happened to those girls. Do you know how they died?'

'I'm afraid not. There are plenty of rumours, of course . . .'

'My interest is only with facts. Who examined the bodies?'

'That was Old Seb, our local Ombudsman. It's his job to examine the deceased of the parish and write weekly reports for the Order.'

'And where can I find him?'

'Ah, well, there's the rub,' Treacher said with a shake of his head. 'Poor Seb's fallen with the plague. He's been in the Pest House for a week, and for all I know he might already be dead.'

10
THE WITCH HUNTER GENERAL

'Witches are like rats: sly, sinful and covered in filth.'
Matthew Hopkins, Witch Hunter General

Hazel and Anthony stood rigidly at attention outside Matthew Hopkins' office. The solid oak door was closed, but they clearly heard the argument raging inside.

'You're failing in your duty, General. The people want him dead.'

'The people do not know what is best for them, John. They never do.'

'That must be Hopkins' voice,' Bramley whispered from under Hazel's new cap.

Hazel supposed so – it certainly sounded cold enough for a man who led a murderous crusade – and she thought she recognized the first voice too.

That's John Stearne, the so-called Witch Butcher who arrested Nicolas Murrell, and it seems he's not afraid to stand up to his master.

She fidgeted in her new uniform. The soft black trousers and shirt were fine, but the boots pinched and the scarlet knee-length jacket itched around her neck. At least the felt cap with the crossed-hammer insignia gave Bramley somewhere else to hide.

'And what of Cromwell?' Stearne continued, his deep voice rumbling with anger. 'If he knew how many witches you're keeping . . .'

'Our Lord Protector entrusted me to look after things here, as I see fit, while he fights the rebels in the North.'

'He expects you to prosecute witches, and get rid of animals like Murrell *tout de suite*.'

'*Tout de suite*?' Hopkins said. 'Oh, John, you *do* surprise me. I didn't know you spoke *French*.'

'I spent three years with the Parisian branch of *La Société des Chasse-Sorcières* before joining the Order.'

'Ah, of course, *la trouvez et brûlez* brigade. No wonder your methods lack subtlety.' Hopkins sighed, like a parent trying to make a truculent child see sense. 'I'm not keeping all those filthy witches alive for fun. I'm doing it so we can learn from them. And imagine what secrets Murrell has! Killing him would be a waste.'

'When a man finds a cockroach he steps on it.'

'And an *educated* man knows that stepping on a cockroach won't always kill it.'

Hazel flinched as Stearne, a lean man built like a bare-knuckle boxer, stormed out of the office and down the corridor. Both Hazel and Anthony craned their necks to see inside Hopkins' office and saw a short, rather plump man standing with his back to them looking out of the window.

If this was Matthew Hopkins, the scourge of English

witches, he was not what Hazel expected.

'Well, boys,' he said without turning round. 'Don't stand there gawping. Come in.'

Anthony paled and looked like he was going to run away. Hazel put a reassuring hand on his shoulder and guided him inside.

'He must have eyes in the back of his head,' Bramley muttered.

The sun glinted on the crossed-hammer emblem on Hopkins' collar as he turned from the window and sat down behind a large oak desk; Hazel noticed how the skin around his fingernails was red raw, as if he'd been chewing it.

He took a few moments to adjust his papers and then looked up at them with a smile that did not touch his cold, blue eyes. The silence stretched until, unable to stand it any longer, Hazel blurted, 'Thank you, General Hopkins. Myself and Anthony feel honoured to have been chosen to serve in the glorious Order.'

Anthony managed a frightened nod.

'Master William Lowe,' Hopkins stated, tapping a piece of paper on his desk. 'Your interrogator informs me that your dominant humour is sanguine: passionate and energetic.'

'I can get quite fiery at times, General,' Hazel replied.

'Good! That's just what we want in the Order – after all, fire is our stock-in-trade, is it not?'

Hazel thought of the execution pyres she'd seen on her journey to London: the drifting piles of ash, the stakes burned down to blackened spikes. Careful to keep the anger out of her voice, she said, 'It certainly is, General.'

'But he also tells me that you're ignorant and uneducated. What have you got to say to that?'

'I may not be as clever as some, General,' she said, unable to control the flash of pique, 'but I'm not stupid.'

Hopkins' smile dropped like a lead weight. 'Is this my first glimpse of your fiery temper, William?'

'Probably best not to shout at the Witch Hunter General,' Bramley hissed.

'My apologies,' Hazel said. 'What I meant to say is that I'm keen to learn and I believe this is the best place for me to do so.'

'We'll see.' Hopkins turned to Anthony, smiling in the way a snake would at a cornered mouse. 'Master Anthony Simpson. You are exactly what I'm looking for. Such angelic features! You are the very picture of childish innocence. Perfect for the special job I have planned for you. But, all in good time, eh?'

Hopkins leaned contentedly back in his chair and clasped his fingers over his stomach. 'William, Anthony, you are now Junior Apprentices in the Grand Order of Witch Hunters. You will report directly to me, but you will also obey the commands of those above you in rank – which in your case is everyone. Understood?'

'Yes, General,' Hazel and Anthony said.

'Good. In return for your loyal and unswerving service, I will ensure you are fed, educated and looked after. I have rooms for you here in the White Tower. Anthony – you told your interrogator that your mother is unwell?'

'Er, yes, General,' Anthony said, looking surprised. 'I want to earn enough to pay an apothecary to—'

Hopkins waved his hand. 'No need. I'm going to send my personal physician to see what he can do for her.'

Anthony's mouth dropped open. 'Th-thank you, General.'

'The Order looks after its own. I'll take you to him right away and you can tell him where she lives.' He got up and headed for the door with Anthony in tow. 'William, I can't abide dust, so clean my office while I'm gone – I want all the surfaces spotless. You'll find a cloth in that drawer there. Come, Anthony.'

Hazel closed the door after them and let out a long, shaky breath.

'Well,' Bramley said, climbing down on to her shoulder. 'He's a box of contradictions, and no mistake.'

Hazel shook her head in consternation. 'How can a monster look so much like a man?'

'I can't *abide* dust,' Bramley said in a good imitation of Hopkins. 'So you'd better get to work, Master Lowe. And have a poke about while you're at it – you might find something about where they're keeping Murrell. Look on his desk, for a start.'

With her back to the door, Hazel leaned over the desk and flipped through a pile of leather folders: *News from Salem, The Lancaster Assizes, The North Berwick Witch Trials*, and finally one that made her heart leap up into her throat.

'*A Concise Report on England's Enemy,*' she breathed. '*Nicolas Murrell.*'

'Oooh! Go on – open it, quick!'

Hazel's gaze strayed to the door. 'It's not like you to encourage such a risk.'

'Huh! We're in the office of the Witch Hunter General. How can things get any more dangerous?'

Inside the folder was a sheaf of papers. The topmost one was a faded poster depicting a rather demonic-looking Murrell.

'Well? What does it say?' Bramley asked.

'*Nicolas Murrell,*' Hazel read. '*Wanted for the Capital Crimes of Demon Worship, Consorting with Witches, Murder and High Treason.*'

She flicked deeper into the pile, skim-reading reports of possible sightings and interrogation transcripts of witches who had known him. 'Hopkins has certainly worked hard to track him down.'

'Is there anything there about where they're keeping him now?'

'Give me a second . . .' Hazel bent lower to decipher some smudged writing. 'There's a lot to go through. Arrest warrants, news pamphlets . . .'

Bramley tensed and crawled slowly back into her hair. 'There's someone behind us. Hazel. *I think it's him!*'

11
OLD SEB

Those blessed with status or money to pay can
convalesce from their affliction in a Pest House.
Plague: A Darke Historie by Dr Louis Székely

The guard looked askance at Titus. 'Let me get this straight – you actually want to go *inside* the Pest House?'

It had been a long, hot walk through the outer districts of Southwark, and the dismal appearance of the Pest House – a large stone building standing alone in the middle of a patch of sun-baked scrubland – had done nothing to improve Titus's mood.

'I do.' He nodded.

'But no one goes in except the plague doctors.'

'Nevertheless, I seek entrance.'

'But *why?*'

'I need to speak to Sebastian Middleton on a most urgent matter. Do you know if he's still alive?'

'The Ombudsman? Just about.'

'Thank God.' Titus held up two gold coins and rubbed them between his finger and thumb. 'So, can I see him?'

The guard shrugged and took the money. 'Your

68

funeral, I suppose. Come with me.'

As Titus went inside he wondered what the unfortunate Pest House residents made of the crossed bones and grinning skulls carved into the eaves and door frame.

The guard stopped at the end of the corridor. 'You can wait in there. I'll see if Seb's well enough to come to you.'

Titus entered a small reception room with moth-eaten tapestries hanging over the walls. Bundles of herbs littered the floor, filling the air with pungent sweetness. He took off his coat and sat by the window, feeling the sun on his back.

I suppose this is better than being locked in your home and left to die, he thought, *but it's still a sorry place for a man to meet his end.*

The door opened and a man with yellow, sweat-greased skin shuffled into the room. He was probably only forty but his sickness had aged him double, and the blankets wrapped around his shoulders were doubtless there to cover any plague buboes he had behind his ears.

Titus had seen plague victims before, and he knew that barring a miracle this man would soon be dead. Hiding his pity, he held out his hand to shake.

The man waved it away. 'Best not, eh?' His voice was phlegmy and every careful movement spoke of his pain, but he peered at Titus with keen blue eyes.

'Sebastian Middleton?' Titus said. 'Southwark's elected Ombudsman?'

'That's me,' he replied, lowering himself into a chair. 'Don't hover about, man. Sit, sit.'

'Thank you.' Titus cleared his throat. 'My name is Titus White, and you have my condolences for your . . . er, condition.'

Seb's laugh sounded like a leaky pair of bellows. 'I'm not dead yet, Mr White, despite appearances. Now, what brings you to see me? I'm intrigued.'

Watching him carefully, Titus said, 'I want to talk about the dead girls.'

For a moment Seb didn't speak, and the two men regarded each other as the groans of the sick filtered through the walls. 'Why do you want to know?'

'I have a ward, a girl about the same age as those who died. I'd like her to be safe on London's streets.'

'I see. And what makes you think you can do anything about it?'

'I have a very particular set of skills,' Titus said, leaning forward. 'Skills I have acquired over a long career that I think will be useful in a case like this.'

'Oh? A career doing what?'

Titus gave a thin smile. 'Witch Finding. Now, are you going to help me put a stop to this?'

Seb scrutinized Titus for a long moment and then settled back in his chair. 'I will.'

'Thank you.' Titus held up his fingers. 'Three victims?'

Seb nodded. 'That I know of.'

'All found in the alleys and backstreets of Southwark?'

'Yes. Orphans, I suppose, about eleven or twelve. Poor, ragged wretches.'

'But child deaths are common, especially during a plague outbreak. Why were these different?' Titus waited as Seb took a rattling breath.

'The poor usually die of disease or starvation, but those girls did not bear the marks of such things – no buboes, no infected wounds. Physically, they seemed reasonably healthy.'

'So you don't know how they died?'

'Oh, I know *how* they died, I just don't know what caused it.'

Titus frowned. 'What do you mean?'

'What I mean, sir, is that those girls died of fright.'

'Fright?'

'Their bodies were stiff and contorted, their eyes and mouths wide open.' His voice lowered to a whisper. 'As if they'd died . . . screaming.'

'God's bones . . . Did you report this to the Order?'

'Of course. I told them something deadly stalks the streets of Southwark and I needed help to investigate.'

'But they did nothing?'

'Not a thing, damn them,' Seb spat. 'But then what do they care about the poor and the destitute?'

'The Order is a plague in itself,' Titus murmured.

'Pirates and murderers, they are.' Seb let out a juddering breath. 'I cling to life with all my strength, Witch Finder, but when I'm gone I will not miss this world we've built.'

'Here, take this.' Titus pulled out his hip flask and put it into Seb's shaking hand. 'And if you remember anything else send a message to Arthur Lowe at the Bannered Mare.'

'Arthur Lowe?'

'Circumstances have forced me to travel incognito.' Titus smiled. 'Farewell, Sebastian.'

'Farewell. And Witch Finder?'

Titus paused by the door. 'Yes?'

'Be careful. Whatever it is out there, I don't think it's a man.'

12
A PROMOTION

'My familiar is a cat night-black – Rare Ted is his name.'
Zoe Lake, the Witch of Blean Common

'**W**hat are you doing?' Hopkins' voice, cold and controlled, spoke right into Hazel's ear.

How did he get behind me without me hearing? she thought wildly. *And did he see Bramley?*

'I asked you a question –' his voice in her other ear now – 'I expect an answer. Face me, William, and explain yourself.'

Hazel turned around and found Hopkins standing so close that she had to lean back against the desk. His soft face was expressionless but the tightness around his lips made Hazel's insides feel watery.

'I was . . . I was dusting, as you asked, General,' Hazel said, trying to control the shake in her voice. Hopkins still didn't move and the desk cut into her back.

His eyes frosted over. 'If you were dusting, then where is your cloth?'

'I was just about to—'

'Never lie to me!' Hopkins shouted. 'Tell me the truth, or I'll feed you to the hounds.'

Hazel whimpered with fear. This short, stout man had no powers like those of the witches and demons she had faced, but his eyes seemed to pierce her soul. *He knows I'm a girl. He knows I'm a witch. He knows everything . . .*

Bramley, now hidden deep in her hair, sent out a pulse of magic. Its warmth spread over her scalp and down her spine.

Hazel took a breath and spoke as calmly as she was able. 'I'm sorry, General, but when I saw the name on that file I couldn't resist taking a look.'

'Which name?' Hopkins hissed.

'Why, Nicolas Murrell – everyone in London is talking about him.'

'Indeed?' Hopkins took a step back.

'Oh yes,' Hazel said. 'They say he's a dangerous criminal, and your star prisoner. I was curious and just wanted a little peek at his file.'

'You know what happened to the curious cat, don't you, William?'

'It got fed to the hounds, sir?'

Hopkins' eyes thawed just a little. He nodded at the folder. 'So you can read. That's unusual for the son of a rat-catcher.'

'My father taught me,' Hazel said, relieved that the larger sum of Hopkins' anger seemed to have passed. 'He said it was important to learn so I could better myself.'

'A shrewd man.' Hopkins leaned past her, shuffled the papers back inside the folder and retied the ribbon.

'I'm truly sorry for looking where I shouldn't,' Hazel said humbly, 'but I've wanted to be a Witch Hunter all my life, and it is my most fervent desire to help the Order in any way I can.'

'What you did was wrong, and what's worse is you allowed me to catch you in the act – you'll need to be cleverer if you want to be a Witch Hunter.' Hopkins drummed his fingers on the folder. 'But I think you are honest at heart. Tell me, William, can you write as well as read?'

Hazel nodded eagerly. 'My penmanship is excellent.'

'Mm, well, it so happens that my scribe has been indisposed and I need someone literate to replace him. Do you think you're up to the task? It won't be easy – you'll be at my side all day, taking notes and transcribing my interrogations.'

Bramley crawled nearer to her ear. 'That means you might get close to Murrell – say yes quickly before he changes his mind.'

Hazel drew herself up to her full height. 'It would be an honour, General.'

'Good. But remember, you're on trial. Fail, and it's back to cleaning duties. Come with me – I want to show you the scribe's room.'

Hazel, still feeling a little wobbly, followed him to the end of the corridor. 'If you don't mind me asking, General, what happened to your last scribe?'

'I regret to say he was hurt badly in the line of duty,' Hopkins said, ushering her into a small room with a desk and a window overlooking the Tower precincts.

Shelves of books and ledgers lined the walls and in the corner was a straw mattress with some blankets piled on top; for a room in the most dreaded building in England, Hazel found it surprisingly cosy.

'What happened to him?' she asked.

'It was during an interrogation. We'd been starving the prisoner, a convicted witch, for weeks and no one had noticed that she had got so thin she was able to slip her hands out of the manacles. Well, she set about poor Gerard with a will, scratching and biting . . .' Hopkins shook his head, looking genuinely upset. 'He's no good to anyone now.'

Hazel's stomach turned as she wondered what dreadful revenge Hopkins had taken on the witch. 'I'm willing to accept the risks if it means furthering the Order's cause,' she said.

Hopkins nodded approvingly and passed Hazel a small roll of parchment secured with a wax stamp. 'This is my official seal. Show it to the guards to gain admission at any of the Tower gates.'

'Can I go to Cromwell Island?' Hazel asked hopefully.

'Not on your own, but you'll be seeing it soon in any case. I'll be conducting an interrogation with none other than Nicolas Murrell tomorrow and it'll be your job to transcribe it. So get some rest, Master Lowe, for soon your work at the Order begins in earnest.'

13

THREE SUMMERS OLD

It is thought animal familiars have extended lives.
Barring accidents, they can survive at least as
long as the witches they accompany.
A Study of Magical Fauna by Dr Neil Fallon

Hazel closed the door to her room and took a shuddering breath. 'We did it. I can hardly believe it.'

The adrenalin that had kept her going soured in her veins, leaving her weak and shivery. All she wanted to do was curl up on the bed and go to sleep.

'I know,' Bramley said, emerging on to her shoulder and giving himself a shake. 'You've done well not to get us killed.'

Hazel looked out of the window at the surrounding walls and the guards patrolling the ramparts. Beyond rose Cromwell Island, a monolithic nightmare in black stone.

'We're in the dark heart of it here,' she said, opening the window and letting the breeze cool her face. 'Oh, Bram, when Hopkins appeared behind us I thought that was it.'

'You talked your way out of it though, didn't you?'

'But what about next time? If I fail . . .'

'You *are* in a jolly mood. Listen, O foolish one, it may not seem like it, but we actually hold quite an advantage over these awful men.' Bramley scrambled down to the windowsill and fixed her with his sternest glare. 'I mean, think about it: who on earth, who in their right mind, would ever imagine that any witch in the world would be stupid, reckless and mad enough to infiltrate the lair of the Grand Order of Witch Hunters?'

'No one, I suppose . . .' Hazel muttered, wrinkling her brow.

'Exactly. Professional Hunters they may be, but the one place in England they are *not* looking for witches is here, within their own ranks. And,' Bramley added with a raised claw, 'I don't know what this says about you, but that monster Hopkins actually seems to hold you in some kind of regard. I think he likes your gumption.' He gave her a friendly nip on the finger. 'I hate to tempt fate, Hazel, but so far we're doing well. So buck up, will you?'

'I'll try. Thanks, Bram.' Hazel sat at the desk and shook out her hair, which still felt odd being so short. 'I hope Titus is all right. I'm beginning to wish I'd said goodbye.'

'He's about a hundred years old – he can look after himself.'

'I suppose . . .' Hazel watched her familiar as he washed his whiskers, the rust-coloured fur on his back lighting up in the sun. 'How old are you, Bram?'

'This is my third summer.'

'And how long do dormice usually live?'

'Ooh, ages.' Bramley stopped washing and gave her a shrewd stare. 'You're worried I'll die before you, aren't you?'

Hazel looked away. 'I am a bit, yes.'

'Well, don't. I've plenty of seasons left in me yet. And we have more pressing things to consider.'

'The interrogation with Murrell tomorrow?' Hazel said, taking off her jacket and rubbing the itchiness from her neck.

'The interrogation, exactly. We've got to get a message to Murrell *before* that happens. If you simply turn up in his cell with Hopkins he's almost certain to recognize you and give you away.'

'Murrell may hate me, Bram, but I don't think he'd turn me over to the Order.'

'Not deliberately, I agree. But he might do it by accident. I mean, he's going to be pretty surprised to see you, isn't he?'

'Oh! You're right.' Hazel felt a chilly tentacle of dread curl around her spine. 'But how can I get to him? The Island is out of bounds.'

'To you, yes, but not to me.'

Hazel stared at him. 'You're not thinking of going there on your own?'

'I'm not happy about it, but I don't think we have a choice.' Bramley settled on to his back legs and smoothed the fur over his ample stomach. 'Besides, I'll be fine – look how small and nimble I am. And I have an excellent sense of direction.'

'Absolutely *not*,' Hazel said, dashing to the window and picking him up. 'Why, the very thought—'

'Hush. It has to be me, and it has to be me *alone*. There's no other way to get a message to that wretched man.'

Tears pricked behind Hazel's eyes. 'No, no, *no*! I won't let you . . . What if you get lost?' She let out a cry of distress. 'Oh, Bram, what if someone *treads* on you?'

'Oh, really!' Bramley pulled himself up to his full two-and-a-half-inch height and puffed out his chest. 'What do you take me for? A dizzy harvest mouse? I can look after myself, thank you very much. I'll hide in shadows and creep under doors and through bars and gates until I find him.' Bramley's voice softened. 'Don't snivel, Hazel – I'll be back before you know it.'

Hazel wiped her nose with her sleeve. 'All right, you foolish, *foolish* mouse.'

'That's better. Now, you'll need to get me as near to the bridge as you can. Time's pressing, so we'd better make a move.'

Hazel held him close to her heart for a moment, then let him crawl up to her shoulder. She put on her cap and jacket and left the office. No one took any notice of her as she made her way down the stairs and through the courtyard.

The Embankment teemed with patrolling soldiers, gossiping officials, and prowling Witch Hunters. Keeping her eyes downcast, Hazel scurried past them all towards the bridge leading to Cromwell Island.

'Hazel, we're trying to be inconspicuous,' Bramley chided. 'I've never seen anyone look so furtive.'

'I *feel* furtive,' Hazel hissed. 'I've never felt furtiver.'

'Take a deep breath, walk slower and add a bit of swagger,' Bramley said, stroking her neck with his tail. 'That's it! Eyes *up*, girl. Nearly there . . .'

Hazel slowed down as she passed into Cromwell Island's shadow. One of the soldiers guarding the bridge looked at her, noted her uniform and turned back to his conversation.

'I think this is as close as I can go,' she said, bending down as if to tie her shoelaces.

'I don't know how long this is going to take,' Bramley said. 'And it's a long way back to your room in the Tower, so I'll meet you back here tomorrow. Come and find me when you can.'

'You'd *better* come back,' Hazel whispered, her voice catching in her throat.

'I will.' Bramley scampered down her arm. 'No one's going to notice a tiny scrap like me, are they?'

Before Hazel had a chance to say goodbye, her little familiar dived into the gutter and scampered off towards the bridge. She wanted to run after him, gather him up and never let him go. Instead she slowly made her way back to the Tower.

Sights and sounds floated past and through her. She didn't feel the sun, or the breeze. All she was aware of through the daze was an aching sense of loss in the pit of her stomach. Bramley had gone, and for all she knew he might never return.

She sped up the stairs, realizing she would not be able to stem the tide any longer – and sure enough, upon reaching her office and closing the door behind her, she slid to the ground and wept bitterly and long into the night.

It was dark when Hazel, red-eyed and puffy-faced, gathered herself and decided to do some reading to keep her mind from worrying about Bramley. Choosing a book called *The Black Library* by Marcus Gascoigne, she lit a lantern and settled down at her desk to while away the hours until morning.

Her eyes were just beginning to feel heavy when the door opened and Hopkins burst in.

'William,' he cried. 'So you couldn't sleep either? Excellent!'

Hazel jumped to her feet. 'General, sir. What time is it? Is everything well?'

'Oh, yes indeed,' Hopkins said, bouncing on the balls of his feet. 'And it's three in the morning. Gather your things, quickly. Ink, quills, paper, and that folding table over there.'

'But where are we going?'

'To interrogate Nicolas Murrell, of course,' Hopkins replied with a grin. 'We're going early – I'm in the mood for torment.'

14
ADMINISTRATIONS

'The Order is a broom to sweep this nation clean.'
Grandee Edward Grimstone

Laden down with fear and a portable writing desk, Hazel followed Hopkins and his two blue-robed clerks across the bridge to Cromwell Island.

Bramley had not been at the spot they had agreed to meet at, which meant he was still inside. Hazel had no way of knowing if he'd managed to warn Murrell that she was in disguise and on her way to see him. Worse still, she had no way of knowing if he was lost, hurt . . . or worse.

He's not dead, she thought, more in hope than certainty. *Surely I'd feel it if he was?*

A heavy door set into the wall to the side of the main double gates opened and a guard stepped out, saluting Hopkins as he and his clerks marched past. Reminding herself that she was doing all this for her mother, Hazel hefted the table more securely under her arm and followed them inside.

A vast circular chamber, wide and tall enough for two sailing ships to sit side by side, opened up around her. The floor was like black ice, smooth, polished and shimmering in the light of a hundred lanterns. Spiralling around the wall to the vanishing ceiling far above was a walkway lined with iron-studded doors. *Those must be cells*, Hazel thought. *And there are so many of them.*

In the centre of the chamber about forty witches in rough prison smocks were shuffling, one behind the other, in an endless circle. Their bare feet were blue with cold, their ankles swollen. The exhaustion on their faces pierced Hazel's heart. Soldiers stood nearby, goading and shouting at any who slowed down or stumbled.

One of the clerks noticed Hazel staring. 'It's called "Witch Walking",' he said. 'Those prisoners will not be allowed to eat, rest or sleep until they confess their sins or give up one of their so-called sisters. It's a very effective method pioneered by the General himself.'

A flush of anger heated Hazel's blood. With an effort she managed to suppress it, but when she turned to the clerk she saw he was frowning. 'What's the matter?' she said, her anger curdling into fear.

'I'm not sure. For a second there you seemed to be . . . *glowing.*'

'Glowing?' Hazel forced a smile. 'Why, whatever can you mean, sir?'

'Oh, must be nothing – a mere trick of the light.' He glanced at Hopkins. 'Come, the General is waiting.'

Hopkins had paused at the foot of the walkway, inhaling deeply like a man enjoying a summer breeze; all Hazel felt was cold air, heavy with the smell of damp stone and misery.

They followed Hopkins along the walkway, round and round, up and up, past locked doors and grim-faced guards, until they reached halfway between the floor and ceiling, and the people below were barely visible in the gloom.

Hopkins stopped outside a door guarded by two soldiers and took a key from his pocket. 'This is the first time I've spoken to Murrell since putting him in the Oven. I wonder if he's feeling more forthcoming now?'

'No one can stand the Oven for long,' one of the clerks said. 'He'll break sooner or later.'

'Perhaps, but we'd do well not to underestimate our opponent.' Hopkins turned to Hazel. 'William, I want you to set up your table in the corner and transcribe my conversation so I can peruse it later. Do you understand?'

'Yes, General.'

'Good.'

Hopkins unlocked the door and beckoning them through. Hazel faltered at the threshold. This could be the moment her endeavour failed – if Murrell gave her identity away then she'd be captured and no doubt killed.

If that happens I'm not going down without a fight.

The cell was small, windowless, and lit with three guttering torches. A stone bench ran along one wall. Tied to a chair in the middle of the room sat a man wearing a filthy horsehair tunic. His face was hidden behind a curtain of black hair, but Hazel recognized him instantly: this was Nicolas Murrell, and she was shocked at how thin he looked.

There was no sign of Bramley, which meant Murrell might not know about her presence. So, hoping to stay out of sight, Hazel crept to the darkest corner, perched on the bench and set up her writing table as quietly as she could.

On Hopkins' cue one of the guards picked up a bucket of water and hurled the contents at Murrell. The force nearly tipped the chair over, and left Murrell gasping for air.

What should I do if they start to hurt him? Hazel thought, laying out some parchment with trembling hands. *I can't hope to rescue him, but can I really sit here and watch his mistreatment?* It was a decision she hoped she would not have to make.

Whistling between his teeth, Hopkins sat on a stool in front of his prisoner and drew a curved blade from his pocket. Hazel tensed as he leaned forward and used it to sweep Murrell's hair away from his face.

'Ah,' he said. '*There* you are.'

'My gracious host.' Murrell's voice cracked, as if he had not spoken for a long time. 'How nice of you to arrange this visit.'

'Oh, it's the least I can do.' Hopkins put the knife away and laced his fingers over his stomach. 'So,' he purred, 'how are you finding the Oven?'

Hazel began to transcribe, struggling to keep her handwriting steady.

'I find the solitude rather soothing,' Murrell replied mildly.

'You lie! I once left a prisoner in there for two days, and

when I let her out she tried to throw herself off the roof.'

'*De gustibus non est disputandum,*' Murrell said, looking up at the ceiling.

Hazel didn't understand the words, but she noticed Hopkins' lips twitch with irritation.

'Rubbish,' he replied. 'The Oven is intolerable for anyone, even a man as sick at heart as you.'

'Yet here I am, hale and hearty.'

'Hale and hearty? You don't look it, Nicolas.'

Hazel could not help but be impressed when, despite his bonds, Murrell managed a carefree shrug.

'Ah, such bravura! Such studied insouciance!' Hopkins smiled. 'It doesn't fool me, of course – I know how you suffer in the heat and the dark. And so you'll be pleased to know that I'm here to offer you some respite.'

Murrell raised his eyebrows. 'Oh? There'll be conditions, I assume?'

'Naturally. You'll have to answer all of my questions honestly, completely and without reservation. Do that and I'll put you in a room in the White Tower with a bed and enough space to stretch your legs.'

And so began an interminable half-hour as Hopkins bombarded Murrell with questions. How many witches had he commanded in his Coven? Where are the rebel safe houses in London? What demon had he treated with when he'd travelled to the Underworld?

Through it all Murrell just stared at the floor and uttered not a single word.

'I know you had Wielders in your Coven – I even know their *names*,' Hopkins said, getting up and walking behind Murrell. 'David, my trusty informant, told us all about them.'

So David has *been talking*, Hazel thought, flexing her aching fingers. *Is he doing so willingly, or is he being tortured too?*

'Lilith Kilbride,' Hopkins continued. 'A Frost Witch you were particularly close to. So far she has eluded us, but we'll find her sooner or later. And then there was a White Witch, a healer, called Hecate Hooper.'

Hazel bit her lip. It felt strange to hear her mother's name spoken by Hopkins.

'She ended up a victim of your dark deeds,' Hopkins said, putting his hands on Murrell's shoulders. 'Stolen into the Underworld by a demon. Still . . .' He shrugged. 'One less Wielder for me to worry about, eh?'

Not if I get her back, Hazel thought.

Hopkins squeezed Murrell's shoulders hard enough to make him wince. 'But she had a daughter. You remember her? Of course you do! Her name is Hazel. She's a Fire Witch, dangerous, and I want to know where she is.'

Startled by the mention of her own name, Hazel pushed a bit too hard on the quill and snapped the nib. Ink spilt all over the parchment. She grabbed a blotter to soak it up.

'This is your last chance to cooperate,' Hopkins said, walking back in front of Murrell. 'If you don't, it's back to the Oven and this time I'll leave you there until you dry up like a slug on a skillet.'

Murrell cleared his throat as if preparing to speak. Hazel held her breath.

'Yes?' Hopkins urged.

Murrell spat on to Hopkins' boot and grinned up at him.

Hopkins grabbed a fistful of Murrell's hair and jerked his head back. 'You may not have broken yet, but I've plenty of time to twist you and turn you until you snap.' He let go and gestured for the guard to open the door. 'Pack up your things, William. This interrogation is over.'

Hazel looked up from the parchment to find Murrell staring directly at her. Her heart raced when she realized that he knew exactly who she was – and if the wry smile he gave her was anything to go by, he'd known from the moment she'd walked into the cell.

As the guards moved in to untie him, Murrell opened his hand and let something drop to the floor. Hazel nearly let out a cry of relief.

It was Bramley, bright-eyed and unharmed, nimbly dodging the boots of the guards as he slid towards her with his belly flat to the ground. The moment everyone's attention was elsewhere, Hazel bent down, picked him up and slipped him into her pocket.

15
HOPKINS CONFIDES

*'I hereby remove all legal hindrances and let my Witch
Hunters govern themselves in their duties.'*
Lord Protector Oliver Cromwell addressing Parliament, 1645

Surrounded by an angry black cloud, Hopkins dismissed his clerks and prowled all the way back to the Tower of London. Hazel followed. She had to use both hands to carry her desk and writing equipment, but she could feel Bramley's weight in her pocket and it lifted her heart higher than it had been for days.

You did it, my clever little mouse! she thought. *I'll never scold you again.*

Hopkins climbed up to the ramparts and looked moodily out over the city. Dawn was breaking and the salmon pink sky heralded another balmy day in London.

The manic energy he'd exuded before the interrogation had been replaced with a brooding preoccupation; Hazel put down the table, slipped her hand in her pocket to give Bramley an affectionate squeeze, and waited.

'Look out there, William,' Hopkins said. 'Tell me what you see.'

'I see the city, General. Houses, churches, the river . . .'

'What else? Down there, in the streets.'

'Er . . . people?'

'People, yes. About six hundred thousand of them, all packed inside these ancient city walls.' His shoulders sagged. 'And while Lord Cromwell fights the rebels in the North they are my responsibility.'

'The people are lucky to have you, General,' she said, quickly lifting Bramley to her shoulder and letting him crawl into her hair.

'The people fear me and call me tyrant – they don't understand that everything I do is to keep them safe.'

Hazel edged closer, wondering why Hopkins was opening up to her like this. *He's tired and disappointed by what happened with Murrell. And perhaps he doesn't have anyone else he can trust to talk to.*

'What of your colleagues within the Order?' she asked.

'Careerists to a man. They resent me – a mere country lawyer raised above my station – and covet my power and closeness to Lord Cromwell. I'm always looking over my shoulder, William. Always.'

Hazel decided to push him a little further. 'You never married, General?'

'Oh, I was married once. I had a son too, about your age. Plague took them both. To my regret I wasn't with them when they passed.'

'I'm . . . sorry,' Hazel said softly.

'It happened. And I am left behind.'

Despite who Hopkins was, despite all the terrible things

he was responsible for, Hazel could not help but feel a stab of pity for him – the pain she heard in his voice mirrored that which she felt at the loss of her mother.

'I'm married to the Order now, for my sins.' Hopkins gathered himself, standing up straight and clasping his hands behind his back. 'And so are you, William! You did well back there.'

'I'm happy to serve,' Hazel said, feeling the lie come smoothly. 'Actually, General, I'd like to ask you a favour, if I may.'

'Oh?'

'It's just I've not had a chance to tell my father that I've been accepted into the Order. He'll be so proud. Can you spare me for an hour or two so I can go and give him the good news?'

Hopkins considered, 'I have an important job for you to do later, but perform it to my satisfaction and I'll give you leave to see your father this evening. Now go to your room and rest. I'll send Anthony when I need you.'

'Yes, General,' Hazel said, suppressing a sigh of relief. 'Thank you.'

16
A MOUSE'S TALE

Ward off plaguey vapours by chewing tobacco, rue or angelica.
Cures for Common Folk by Rachel Kellehar

Hazel rattled back to her room with the table under her arm. After closing the door she sat down and placed Bramley on the desk.

'Are you hurt?' she said, running her hands over his fur. 'Oh, Bram, I missed you! I'm never letting you do anything like that again.'

'I'm fine, no need to fuss.' He puffed up with pride. 'Did rather well, didn't I?'

'Right now, little mouse, I believe you can do anything.' Hazel grinned. 'What did Murrell say about me going to the Underworld to rescue Ma?'

Bramley held up a paw. 'All in good time. First I need something to eat. I'm *starving*.'

Deciding it was the very least he deserved and realizing that she was also hungry, Hazel dashed to the kitchens on the ground floor and loaded a plate up with bread, cheese, hot cuts of meat, and the two nicest apples she could find.

When she returned, her dormouse-familiar was fast

asleep on the blotter with his tail curled over his head. Hazel woke him, then cut up the apple.

'So,' she said after they'd eaten, 'now you can tell me what happened.'

Bramley sat up on his hind legs and began. 'It was a dark and stormy night, and the rain fell in torrents—'

'No it didn't! It was a perfectly nice evening. Now come on, mouse, don't exaggerate.'

'You've got no imagination, that's your trouble,' Bramley muttered. 'So, after you let me go, I made my way across the bridge, moving like a tiny shadow past the guards. While I waited for someone to open the door a beady-eyed seagull was watching me, probably wondering what dormouse tastes like. Luckily a troop of guards came out and I sneaked inside before he got a chance to get me.'

'Were you scared?' Hazel asked, eyes wide.

'Of course! And you've not even heard the half of it. Next thing I had to do was find out where they were keeping Murrell, so I overcame my fear and found a guardroom.'

'How did you stay hidden?'

'I stayed close to the walls –' he flattened himself to the desktop and used his back legs to wriggle forward – 'and moved all the way like this.'

'Clever mouse!' Hazel said, hiding a smile behind her hand.

Bramley continued in hushed tones. 'In the guardroom were some scraps of food, so, braving the risk of discovery, and despite the fact I don't very much care for it, I managed to fortify myself with some cheese.'

Hazel rolled her eyes.

'I was *hungry*.' He lowered his voice even more. 'And then, a stroke of luck! The guards started talking about a "top secret prisoner". *They must mean Murrell*, I thought from my vantage point in a milk jug. I waited for ages, and then an order from Hopkins came through, saying they were to prepare the "top secret prisoner" for interrogation straight away.'

'So what did you do?'

'I did my special creeping walk along the floor, climbed on to one of the guard's boots and held on for dear life as he marched off to carry out the order.'

'So you rode all the way to where they're keeping Murrell?' asked Hazel in awe.

'I did – on the roof. And would you believe there's a garden there? It belongs to Hopkins and he tends it himself.'

'Hopkins has a garden at the top of the Island? How strange.'

'It's quite nice, in an orderly, regimented kind of way. Anyway, the place where they're keeping Murrell is this tiny little room with no windows, and when the guards opened the door I dashed inside.' Deciding to keep Hazel in suspense for a while, Bramley began to gnaw on a slice of apple.

'Bram!' Hazel said, tapping him on the nose. 'Hopkins might call for me any moment, so come *on*.'

'All right . . . So, this room was terrible – roasting hot –

and Murrell was all crouched up and shaky, but as soon as he saw me he snatched me up and said, "I know you, you're *hers*!"' Bramley looked up at her with his bright black eyes. 'He meant you, and I was terrified because he hates you, and one squeeze and he could have killed me.'

'Did you explain what you were doing there?'

'I couldn't. He kept me in his hand while the guards grabbed him and marched him to that cell and tied him to the chair. Luckily they left him there alone – either because he scared them or because he smelt so horrible – and we got a few minutes to talk.'

'What did you say?'

'I managed to tell him you were here, disguised as an apprentice, and you needed to speak to him about Hecate. Then the guards came back so I hid in his hand.' Bramley climbed up her arm and rubbed against her neck. 'He hid me until you were leaving, then he let me go.'

'And he didn't give me away . . .'

'You were right – as much as he resents you, he'd never betray a witch to the Order. But I have to say, I doubt he'll agree to help us without getting something in return.'

'Such as?'

'Rescue, of course – what else?'

'But he knows that's impossible,' Hazel said, tugging nervously on a strand of hair.

'He's also got nothing to lose, so he'll probably demand it anyway.'

'Well, whatever the case may be I need to talk to him

properly. At least Hopkins is committed to keeping him alive, so we've got time to find a way . . .'

The door opened and Hazel managed to sweep Bramley into her pocket just as Anthony poked his head in.

'Hello, William,' he said. 'The General wants you right away.'

'Oh, right,' Hazel replied. 'Coming.'

There was an unusual hush in the corridor as they hurried towards Hopkins' office. Hazel saw two men – one middle-aged, the other old and stooped over a cane, both wearing long black cloaks – conferring together at the top of the stairwell.

'Who are they?' Hazel whispered.

'They're Grandees,' Anthony replied. 'The old one is known as the Spymaster – he's terrifying. There's to be a meeting with them all right now. That's what the General wants you for.'

They hesitated on the threshold of Hopkins' office. Light streamed through the floor-length window, silhouetting Grimstone – tall, severe, hat tucked under his arm, and Hopkins – head bowed, feet firmly planted, hands clasped behind his back.

'And Stearne?' Hopkins was saying. 'Is he gracing us with his presence at the meeting today?'

'Captain Stearne's not been seen since your conversation yesterday.' Grimstone drew a letter from his pocket. 'Although my spies intercepted this – a dispatch from him to Lord Cromwell.'

Hopkins raised an ironic eyebrow. 'Singing my praises, I presume?'

'He's telling Lord Cromwell you lack the stomach for the job, that you're *weak*. And keeping Murrell and all those witches alive only serves to add fuel to his arguments.'

'I'm keeping them alive so I can learn how better to fight them.'

'I know that, but most of the Grandees don't agree. They want the vermin exterminated right now —' Grimstone lowered his voice — 'and if he were here, Cromwell would want the same.'

'Bloody fools!' Hopkins snatched the letter from Grimstone and tore it up. 'Now is not the time to waver from our path. Murrell is close to breaking and damn it all, I'm still master of this house. I'll set the Grandees straight this very day.'

Hazel would have liked to hear more, but Anthony cleared his throat to alert the Witch Hunters to their presence.

Grimstone turned to leave. 'At least set a date for Murrell's execution, General. That might mollify the Grandees for a while.'

'Anthony, go with Sir Grimstone,' Hopkins said, beckoning Hazel forward. 'I trust you are rested, William? Good. I am about to chair a meeting with the Grandees of the Order, and I'd like you to be there.'

'Of course, General,' Hazel said. 'Can you tell me my duties?'

'You are there to attend to me, but in the main I'd like you to be an observer.'

'An observer?'

'Indeed,' Hopkins said, tidying up some loose papers on his desk. 'Careful observation is an important aspect of Witch Hunting.'

'That sounds like the sort of thing Titus would say,' Bramley whispered.

'Very well, General,' Hazel said. 'And the Grandees . . . ?'

'They are my esteemed and learned colleagues who, under my auspices, run the various aspects of the Order. There's the Custodian of Records, the Auditor of Coin, the Spymaster, the Guardian of the Law, and the Warden of the Gaols.' He shook his head. 'And a more intractable, vicious, backstabbing lot you would not wish to meet, William. Grimstone is the only one I trust.'

'And Captain Stearne?'

'My deputy, and the worst of them all.' Hopkins grimaced. 'Lord Cromwell's appointment, not mine.'

'I shall be your eyes and ears, General.'

'Good. Now, I think I've kept them waiting long enough.' Hopkins straightened his jacket. 'Always arrive last to a meeting, William – it shows everyone where the power lies.'

'Time to face the hyenas, Hazel,' Bramley whispered. 'Just try to stay inconspicuous.'

17
THE GRANDEES GATHER

'It's always later than you think.'
Titus White

The guards at the open double doors stood to attention as Hopkins and Hazel swept into the conference room. The six men around the oak table rose and bowed their heads – all except the old man Anthony had identified as the Spymaster. He remained seated, scowling, gnarled hands curled over his walking cane.

'These must be the Grandees,' Bramley whispered as Hazel followed Hopkins to the other end of the table.

And what a grim bunch they are, Hazel thought, standing to the left of Hopkins' high-backed chair.

The Grandees wore a more elaborate variation of the simple black Witch Hunter uniform, and their cloaks were fastened with personalized silver clasps: a key for the Warden of the Gaols, a silver penny for the Auditor of Coin, a quill for the Custodian of Records, a keyhole for the Spymaster, a pair of scales for the Guardian of the Law, and a sword for Grimstone, the Recruitment Sergeant.

Hopkins placed his hands flat on the table. 'I see Captain Stearne has not graced us with his presence. Never mind, we will continue *in absentia.*'

'He's on his way.' The Spymaster's voice was dry as dust. 'We should wait.'

Hopkins lowered his tone. 'We shall proceed.'

'Very well,' the Spymaster replied. 'Then let's begin with the upcoming Execution Pageant. My fellow Grandees and I are interested to know how many prisoners you are planning to execute.'

Hazel saw Grimstone and Hopkins exchange the briefest of glances; the meeting was already going just as they had expected.

'I've selected six witches who have been squeezed of all the information they have,' Hopkins said. 'They shall be burned in front of a chosen audience of allies in the Tower Hill arena.'

'Six?' the Spymaster spat. 'We should be burning six hundred, not six. And what about that animal Murrell? He needs to be dealt with . . . permanently.'

'As I've repeated many times before, Murrell has vital information that will allow us to fight witches more effectively.'

'And what information has he given you so far?' the Master of Coin asked.

'I'll tell you myself – none!' the Spymaster crowed. 'He's not spoken a word since brave Captain Stearne apprehended him.'

'I think that Spy-man is even worse than Hopkins,' Bramley muttered.

Hazel saw Hopkins clench his jaw. *He's going to lose his temper any second . . .*

'He should be executed at the Pageant,' another Grandee stated against a backdrop of approving murmurs. 'The people demand it . . .'

Hopkins stood up and slammed both fists down on the table. *'I am the master of this house!'* Every Grandee, even the Spymaster, fell silent. 'Appointed by Lord Cromwell to act as his proxy while he fights the rebels in the North. And it is my decision to keep Murrell alive for the time being. Is that understood?'

The Grandees exchanged whispers and nodded their reluctant agreement. Hazel would have felt relieved that Murrell had gained a stay of execution, but the Spymaster's thin smile made her uneasy.

'Well then,' Hopkins said. 'Now that's settled we can get on with the business of the . . .'

Everyone turned as the door opened and Captain Stearne strode in, brandishing a rolled-up parchment.

'Ah-ha! The prodigal son returns,' the Spymaster cried, his wrinkled face creasing further into a satisfied smile.

'Forgive my late arrival, gentlemen,' Stearne said, 'but I have a message from Lord Cromwell.' He grinned wolfishly at Hopkins. 'Do I have the Chair's permission to read it out?'

Hopkins nodded and sat down, looking ready to explode like a misfiring mortar.

Stearne unrolled the parchment and began to read. 'General Hopkins, my loyal Grandees, it is my command that all witches held in the Order's custody, including the wretch Nicolas Murrell, are to be executed as soon as possible.' He looked Hopkins in the eye. 'All witches, and Murrell, as soon as possible. Lord Cromwell himself demands it.'

Hopkins simmered in a white-hot rage as the Grandees decided how best to carry out Lord Cromwell's orders. In the end they decided that all the captive witches would be executed together during the Pageant in a spectacular public display, with the burning of Nicolas Murrell taking place on Tower Hill.

The cold and practical way these men discussed the deaths of so many people sickened Hazel to her core, but all she could do was stand still and listen.

Unease gnawed at her. If Murrell was to die at the Pageant, that left her only a few days to speak to him. And how would he react when he found out he was doomed? Would that make him more or less likely to help her?

It was mid-afternoon when the Grandees concluded the meeting and departed to organize the now far more ambitious Execution Pageant, leaving Hopkins, Grimstone and Hazel behind.

Grimstone closed the conference room door and let out a long breath. 'That could have gone . . . better.'

'Humbugged! Stearne's *humbugged* me, by God!'

Hopkins cried. 'I must break Murrell before the Pageant – if he gives up just a shred of information it might be enough to convince Cromwell that he's too valuable to kill.'

'Then let's go back to the old methods,' Grimstone said. 'Thumbscrews, the rack . . .'

Hazel raised her hand. 'Excuse me, sirs, may I speak?' Both men looked surprised, as if they'd forgotten she was there. 'I was just thinking that if Murrell finds out he's to be executed he'll have nothing to lose, and you'll *never* get him to talk.'

'So?' Grimstone said.

'So,' Hazel continued, 'if you let him out of the Oven to be, um, *administered* to, he might get wind of it and clam up forever.'

Hopkins considered her words. 'The boy's right, Grimstone. And in any case, such methods have never worked on Murrell before. For now we'll keep him contained in the Oven and ensure we are the only ones to speak to him. It's still a few days until the Pageant and a lot may happen in that time.'

'Very well, General,' Grimstone said. 'If you'll excuse me, I'd better return to my duties.'

'At least you've saved Murrell from being tortured,' Bramley whispered. 'But we still have to get a message to him.'

Hazel needed time away from the confines of the Tower, and was desperate to confer with Titus about everything that had happened.

'General,' she said. 'Would now be convenient for me to visit my father? You said I could if I performed my duties to your satisfaction.'

'Yes, off you go,' Hopkins said, staring distractedly out of the window. 'But be back first thing tomorrow morning.'

'I will, General. Thank you.' Hazel headed gratefully for the door.

18
THORN

In England, the robin (Erithacus rubecula) *is considered lucky.*
An English Phantasmagoria by Dr Lee Dorian

The rider stood in the stirrups of his rearing horse, sword raised and ready to strike. Three hag-like witches cowered beneath, their faces twisted with fear.

'What a horrible statue,' Bramley said from behind Hazel's ear.

After leaving the Tower, Hazel had spotted a deserted public garden with flowers and a fountain tucked away near the river embankment. The early evening sun was hot and the thought of tackling the hordes on London Bridge was too much, so she'd decided to have a rest for a while.

'I think it's supposed to be Hopkins,' Hazel replied, sitting by the fountain and running her hands through the water.

'Huh. It's not very accurate – he's much fatter than that, and his nose is . . .' Bramley trailed off. 'Er, Hazel?'

Hazel had her eyes closed and her face turned to the sun. 'What is it, mouse?' she murmured.

'I'm not sure. I think you'd better see for yourself – over there, by that hedge.'

Hazel saw a one-legged robin staring at her with bright, intelligent eyes. 'Why, it's only a . . .' She gasped as the robin fluttered into the air and landed on her shoulder. Bramley squeaked, retreated, and reappeared on her other shoulder.

'Are you Hazel Hooper the Fire Witch?' The robin spoke with a voice so musical it made Hazel's heart flutter with delight.

'That depends on who's asking.' Bramley bristled.

'My name is Thorn,' the robin replied. 'I am Nicolas Murrell's familiar.'

Hazel plucked the robin from her shoulder, feeling his downy breast, the sharp edges of his wing feathers, and the fragile bones underneath. 'How can that be?' she hissed. 'Murrell's no witch, and only witches have familiars.'

'It's a demon!' Bramley squeaked and dived back into Hazel's hair.

'I'm a common robin – no more, no less.'

Hazel looked into Thorn's shining eyes and then set him down on her lap. 'I believe you, but I'd still like an explanation.'

'Nicolas Murrell may not be a witch in the true sense,' Thorn said, ruffling up his feathers, 'but years of study and his foray into the Underworld have lent him some aspects of witchiness – including the ability to take on a willing and sympathetic familiar.'

Bramley re-emerged. 'You mean you've *agreed* to be his

familiar? He's not bound you with some vile spell?'

'No spell. We met in the garden atop that stone tower in the river,' Thorn said. 'I sensed the torment in his soul, so when he asked for my help, I agreed.'

'So you talk to Murrell, just as I do with Bramley?' Hazel breathed. 'Even when he's in the Oven?'

'I do,' Thorn nodded solemnly. 'There's a gap in the bricks big enough for me to slip through. He asked me to look out for you when he returned from the interrogation. I am glad to have found you at last, Hazel Hooper.'

'So am I,' Hazel said, feeling this bit of good luck was long overdue.

'Don't count your chickens yet, Hazel.' Bramley shook an accusing claw at Thorn. 'Tell us, *bird*, what does your unholy master have to say to us?'

Thorn stretched out a wing. 'He knows why you risked your lives to speak to him.'

'Oh *does* he?' Bramley said.

'Of course. There can only be one reason: you need his help to rescue Hecate Hooper from the Underworld.'

'Yes! *Yes!*' Hazel leaned closer. 'And will he? He should do – after all, it's his fault it happened in the first place.'

'Nicolas wishes to atone for his part in your mother's fate,' Thorn said. 'And to do that you need to speak with him, face to face.'

'But there's no need to,' Bramley said. 'He can just tell you, his own little feathery servant, how to open a gate into the Underworld, and you can pass the information on to us.'

'Exactly,' Hazel said. 'We can meet back here after you've spoken to him . . .'

'Face to face,' Thorn repeated. 'Nicolas says it's the only way.'

Hazel looked helplessly at the earnest little robin, feeling all her hope drain away. 'But I don't think I can get to him . . .'

'Hazel Hooper – you have a loyal and courageous familiar, and according to Nicolas your mother's strength of mind. I doubt not that you can achieve anything you set your mind to.' Thorn hopped on to Hazel's hand and stroked his wings against her skin. 'Goodbye. Nicolas is looking forward to seeing you again.'

19
FACE AGAINST THE GLASS

*The wall between our world and the demons' is paper thin,
and the tears are beginning to show.*
Divinations of Oblivion by Brentford Hinds

Hazel was so deep in thought as she trekked back to the tavern that she didn't even notice people giving her a wide berth when they saw her Witch Hunter's uniform. Indeed, so wrapped up was she that it took Bramley to remind her to take it off before arriving back at the Bannered Mare.

'That's a conversation you really don't want to have with old Treacher,' he said. 'And keep your hair tucked into your cap – you don't want him noticing how short it is.'

Safely changed into her boy's clothes – which she could explain away as her rat-catcher work outfit – Hazel took the back steps into the tavern. There was no sign of Titus, so she returned to her room and locked the door. On her pillow was a note written in a painstakingly neat hand.

'It's from Mr Treacher,' she said.

Bramley peered over her shoulder. 'What does it say?'

Dear Lizzie,

I am writing this in case you return
late and I do not see you. I am pleased
to tell you that the girl you found has
recovered and seems none the worse for
wear from her encounter, of which she
remembers nothing. Mrs Treacher and I
have committed ourselves to looking after
her from now on. I am also heartened to
say that your good father has decided to
investigate the matter of the children's
deaths, having confided in me about his
'previous occupation'. There is food in the
kitchen if you are hungry.

Yours sincerely,
Henry Treacher

'The old Witch Finder is as good as his word,' Bramley
yawned as he clambered on to Hazel's lap and curled up
into a ball. 'I wonder what he's found out?'

Hazel tugged on her bottom lip. 'I hope he comes back
soon. I must speak to him before I leave for the Tower in
the morning.'

'Don't worry, little witch. I'll stay awake and listen out
for his return while you get some . . .' He trailed off and
began to snore.

Hazel let him sleep. As usual when she was alone with her thoughts, they turned to her mother and the terrible place where she was trapped. On the journey to London, Hazel had read Titus's books to learn as much as she could about the Underworld, but she struggled to understand the many theories and contradictory ideas put forward by the demonologist authors.

Some said the Underworld existed beneath the crust of the earth, and that demons looked up enviously at the human world and sought to destroy it. Others said that demons were the souls of the damned made flesh. In the end Hazel had decided that none of those long-dead scholars knew anything for certain.

She had wanted to read the works of Lars Göran Petrov, the demonologist who had travelled to the Underworld many years ago only to be trapped there and used as a slave by Baal, the same demon that now held Hecate. But Titus had told her the *Häxan Jägares* – Swedish Witch Hunters – had destroyed every last copy of his books.

Which left Nicolas Murrell the only man alive with any authority on the subject. *And even if I find a way to speak to him, he cannot be trusted.*

Hazel sighed. Being apart from Titus for the last few days had made her realize how much she had come to depend on his wisdom and strength; he might be a bad-tempered drunk but he was her friend, and she trusted him.

Where are you? she thought, before exhaustion overcame her and she drifted off to sleep.

Hazel woke up groggy and cold on top of the bedclothes – it was dark outside and the tavern was silent. Feeling the need for a breath of air, she left Bramley asleep on the pillow and went to the window.

Titus must not be back yet, she thought. *If he were, surely he'd have looked in to see if I'd returned?*

She threw back the curtain.

A face of cracked leather and stitches stared back at her, so close to the other side of the glass that Hazel saw her own terrified reflection in each round eye. The hideous beak, the hunched spine, the filthy robe . . . It was the attacker from the alley.

A scream rose in Hazel's throat as it pressed a gloved hand against the window. The glass creaked in its frame and then the latch snapped. Hissing with triumph, the creature forced the window inwards and stepped into the room, the top of its hat scraping the ceiling as it advanced.

Hazel stumbled away and tripped on the edge of the carpet. Her world exploded with pain as she cracked her head on the iron bedstead.

Through a swirling fog of disorientation she saw the creature peel off a glove and flex its naked fingers: long, thin, clicking like a faulty clock. No skin, no flesh, just bone. The air curdled with a smell of rancid milk.

This isn't a man, this is a demon . . .

Hazel searched her heart for magic, for a spark of fire to use as a weapon, but it was as if the invader gave off an

113

invisible vapour which doused her will to fight. She let out a whimper and shrank back against the bed.

The creature bent over her, its beaked mask inches from her face – what horrors were concealed inside? Hazel caught a whiff of bitter herbs as it entwined a skeletal finger through a lock of her hair . . .

'Red Witch,' it hissed through the mask. *'Mine now!'*

A tiny fireball trailing smoke leaped off the bed and landed on the demon's beak. 'Get off her!' It was Bramley, consumed in a cocoon of his own burning magic.

Startled, the demon flinched and withdrew, eyes reflecting fire like two gold sovereigns. Its hold over Hazel broke and she rolled out from under its shadow, looking this way and that for a weapon. Bramley dug his claws in tighter, lit nose to tail with flickering tongues of flame.

I can't use magic here, Hazel thought. *I'll set the whole place alight*.

Close to panic, she grabbed a chamber pot from under the bed. She edged closer, waiting for the moment to strike . . .

The demon's floor-length cape flailed as it thrashed its head from side to side in an effort to dislodge the tenacious dormouse. At last Bramley lost his grip and spun through the air like a miniature comet, landing with a squeak in the fireplace's ash pile.

Fury grabbed Hazel. Mustering all of her strength, she let fly with the chamber pot. It struck the demon on the side of the face and shattered, sending broken shards of

114

china in every direction. The demon gave a muffled cry and dropped to one knee.

I could run, Hazel thought, *but what about everyone else in the tavern? Perhaps this thing has come back for the beggar girl! I can't leave them behind in danger . . .*

The sight of Bramley jumping out of the fireplace, covered in ash and baring his teeth, made up her mind: she had to fight, use her magic if she had to, and hope not to set the building on fire.

The creature hissed like a serpent and twisted its body towards her, head low and thrust forward, close enough to see shards of china embedded in the leather. Hazel dredged deep and found a spark. She drove it down her arms until pale flames flickered from her skin. It was weak, barely enough to warm the air, but it was the best she could do as she turned side on and prepared to wield.

Heavy footsteps echoed from the corridor, getting rapidly closer. Someone must have heard the commotion and was coming to investigate. Instinctively Hazel turned to the door and cried, 'Don't come in here!'

The handle rattled. 'Hazel, are you all right? Open the door, will you?'

Titus!

Relief flooded through her as she scrambled to unlock the door, expecting any second to feel the demon's bony fingers encircle her neck. She hauled the door open, but by the time Titus burst inside the demon had gone, leaving the window swinging from its hinges and a whisper, just for her, drifting in the air: '*Red Witch . . . I will find you . . .*'

Titus took in the ash-covered Bramley and Hazel's ravaged expression of fear and said, 'So, care to explain what's been going on?'

Hazel rushed to Bramley and picked him up. 'Are you hurt?' she cried. 'Speak to me, mouse!'

'Urgh! I'm filthy,' he choked, shaking his fur. 'You'll have to give me a bath.'

'Hazel, what's happened?' Titus sniffed the air. 'And why can I smell magic?'

'Wait a second . . .' Hazel poked her head out of the window. The balcony and the alley below were empty; the demon had gone. She let out a shuddering breath, went to Titus and wrapped her arms around his waist. 'I don't think I've ever been so pleased to see you.'

'Be off with you, girl,' Titus said gruffly. 'And tell me everything.'

20

A BRIEF CONFERENCE

*'I hear the Black Widow has returned from exile
to fight the Order. God speed to her.'*
A. A. Hancock, Laird of Glen Sporran

'"**R**ed Witch . . . I will find you,"' Titus repeated after Hazel had told him everything that had happened since they'd parted. 'I don't like the sound of that.'

'It was like it knew me,' Hazel said, shuddering at the memory.

'It must remember you from the alley,' Bramley said from his perch on the bedstead. 'And it came back to get revenge on you for rescuing the girl.'

'Maybe,' Hazel said. 'But it felt like more than that.'

'You've seen it twice, and close up this time,' Titus said, gazing at the London lights across the river. 'What do you think it is?'

'It's wearing a mask so I couldn't see its face,' Hazel replied, running her fingers over Bramley's ash-covered fur. 'But I'm certain it's a demon.'

Old Seb said as much, Titus thought. *If I didn't know better I'd say we were cursed with bad luck.*

'I agree with Hazel,' Bramley added. 'It's much too tall to

be a man – we told you that after we saw it the first time.'

'But demons this size do not just *appear* in our world, they have to be summoned by someone who knows what they're doing,' Titus said. 'And why is it hunting children?'

'Not just any children,' Bramley said. 'It's after Hazel now.'

'I never thought I'd say this,' Titus said, 'but the sooner you get back to the Tower the better. It's the safest place from this creature that I can think of.'

'I'm due back first thing tomorrow, and somehow I've got to find a way to speak to Murrell.'

'You've proved yourself to be resourceful so I'm sure you'll find a way. But have a care, especially around this Thorn creature – any animal associated with Murrell is not to be trusted.'

'We'll be careful,' Bramley said. 'What are you going to do in the meantime?'

'I'm a Witch Finder – what do you think I'm going to do?' Titus replied, checking the firing mechanism of his pistol. 'I'm going to go and look for this murderous demon.'

'What, *now*?'

'Absolutely.'

Hazel leaped up. 'Then I'm coming too.'

'No, no, *no*.' Titus pushed her back on to the chair. 'You're to stay here and rest. You'll need all your wits about you tomorrow in that den of wolves.' He paused by the door. 'I'm glad to see you safe and well, Hazel. Make sure you stay that way.'

Hazel lay on the bed, deep in thought with Bramley napping on the pillow next to her. She was worried about Titus. He looked tired, and thinner than when they had first met.

All the worry and guilt is taking its toll. Is he still strong enough to hunt a demon? I'm not sure that he is.

She looked at Bramley – sensible, sane Bramley – and gently shook him awake. 'Hey, little mouse. I want to ask you a favour, which I'm afraid you're not going to like very much . . .'

21
BRING OUT THE DEAD

Tempus edax rerum ('*Time, that devours all things*')
Ovid, *Metamorphoses*

The sky was clear and the stars cold as Titus took the steps down from the balcony. No sound except the lapping of the low-tide river and the bump and clump of moored boats broke the silence. The demon could be miles away by now, or lying in wait around the next corner.

Years of experience had taught Titus to focus his mind beyond fear, but these days the nagging voice inside that said he was too tired, too old, too *weak* to be any use was getting harder to ignore.

'Shut your yap,' he muttered. 'I'm stronger than most men half my age, and smarter too.'

An empty sherry keg lay in the middle of an alley leading away from the river. Had it simply unbalanced from the stack against the tavern wall? Or had it been *knocked*?

Titus crept past it and squinted into the deserted darkness. Even at this hour they'd usually be some people about: the last drunkard standing being thrown out of a tavern lock-in; the poorest citizens picking through piles of refuse; the local militia on patrol. But there was no one. Not a single soul except him.

Everyone knows about the dead girls, and they're too frightened to come out at night.

The fact that the demon – or whatever it was – had returned to the tavern concerned Titus greatly. Had it come back to kill the beggar girl? Or had it come back for Hazel? It called her the 'Red Witch', so it knew about her magic. Was that why it hunted her?

Keeping to the deepest shadows, Titus made his way up the alley, alert, quiet, and with his pistol at the ready. Gutter muck softened his footsteps. His breath misted in the cold night air.

All the victims had been about the same age as Hazel, and the beggar girl's hair was a similar shade of red. Coincidence? Titus thought not. He saw a *pattern*. And if it was a demon he sought, then someone had summoned it and set it loose on its murderous mission.

And when I get my hands on them they'll be sorry they were ever born.

Titus sidestepped into a doorway when he heard a rumbling, creaking sound coming from a sidestreet ahead. It was getting louder. Yellow lantern light painted the walls, then spilt on to the cobbles, startling a rat which squeaked and ran over Titus's boot.

His hands were steady as he raised his pistol, cocking it slowly to ensure the click wasn't audible. There was a swish of leather and then a shadow appeared on the opposite wall: human-shaped but elongated, with a wide-brimmed conical hat and a long, beak-like nose.

Titus held his breath, raised the pistol and curled his finger around the trigger. Was this Hazel's demon?

A figure wearing a hat and a floor-length robe stopped at the junction six paces from where Titus hid, and turned back the way it had come. Its face was hidden behind a grotesque leather mask, shaped like the head of a bird, nightmare born; there was not an inch of skin visible under the get-up. The lantern it held flashed in flat, circular eyes.

'Come on, Patrick, hurry up,' it said, voice muffled through the mask. 'I want to get back before the next century if you don't mind.'

A shorter figure in identical garb appeared, struggling to push a handcart up the slope. Three plague-riddled corpses lay in the cart, bouncing up and down with every jolt. 'Instead of moaning why don't you give me a hand?'

'Because I'm carrying the lantern . . .'

Titus watched as the uncanny figures and their gruesome cart rattled away, crying in unison, 'Bring out your dead! Bring out your dead!'

He lowered his pistol, letting out the breath he didn't realize he'd been holding.

Those men were plague doctors, employed by the city to pick up victims of the disease and take them to the burial pits. And now Titus knew that the killer was wearing one of their uniforms – the leather robe, beaked mask and hat that Hazel had described.

It made perfect sense: what better disguise was there to allow a killer to move unmolested through a city at night? And what better way to keep a demonic face hidden?

Titus smiled. Now the hunt was really on.

22
SPLICING

'The Anesidora, if she could speak,
would have a strange tale to tell.'
Edward Lloyd, coffee-house owner

Hecate Hooper's voice echoed through the trees, far away and full of fear.

Hazel, my darling daughter – where are you?

Hazel followed it, beating a path through tangled roots and low branches, her breath rasping from her throat. On she went, until she stumbled on to a vast plain bathed in blood-red light. A jagged canyon spouting sulphurous smoke stretched before her, and it was from its bottomless depths that her mother's voice cried.

When Hazel awoke, her pillow was wet with tears. *I'm coming, Ma*, she thought. *Just hold on a little longer.*

It was early, but the sun was already bright in a cobalt sky. Leaving Bramley asleep in a fold of the bedspread, Hazel got dressed. Black breeches, black shirt, crimson jacket, boots tightly laced: her courage grew with every garment she put on. She had fooled the Witch Hunters with layer upon layer of lies, and this uniform was her armour of deceit.

She blew gently on Bramley to wake him up (causing a

sleepy protest) and carried him into Titus's room. Relieved to find the old Witch Finder safe and well and snoring in his chair, she gave him a shake.

'Wha . . . What's happening . . . ?' Titus surfaced by increments and when he eventually managed to focus on Hazel he gave a start and bellowed, 'Good God, what hellish imp is this I see before me?'

Hazel remembered it was the first time he had seen her in the Order uniform. 'It's all right, it's just me – Hazel.'

'In her William-the-Witch-Hunter disguise,' Bramley added.

'I thought the Order had sent their tiniest member to arrest me,' Titus growled, rubbing his eyes. 'Hateful get-up.'

Hazel straightened the sleeves of her jacket. 'I think it's rather smart, and it's got inside pockets which are very useful.'

'But what it *represents* is—'

'I know, I know,' Hazel said, raising her hands. 'I'm only teasing.'

'Very funny.' Titus submerged his head in the washbasin.

'So what happened last night?' Hazel asked when he re-emerged. 'I take it you didn't find the demon?'

'No,' he replied, 'but I did find out something interesting about your night prowler, demon or otherwise . . .' He told Hazel and Bramley about the plague doctors he had encountered, but left out his worry that even if the killer was not targeting Hazel personally, it was targeting girls just like her.

125

'So the leather mask and the robe work as a disguise,' Hazel said.

'Aye, a good one too.' Titus grinned. 'And what's more, it's a *lead*! I'm going to talk to the Plague Doctor Guild Master and see what I can dig up.'

'What makes you think he'll talk to you?' Bramley asked.

'Oh, he'll talk all right, when I tell him the killer stalking these streets is wearing one of his men's uniforms.' Titus scraped the hair away from his face. 'You know, it feels *good* to be investigating again.'

'I'm glad to hear it.' Hazel cleared her throat. 'And perhaps it would be even better if you had some help.'

'Help?' Titus looked blank. 'What sort of help?'

'Oh, you know, like a companion.' Hazel held Bramley out on the palm of her hand.

'What's she talking about?' Titus growled to Bramley.

'Hazel thinks it would be good for us to work together for a while.'

Titus folded his arms. 'But I don't *like* company. It gets in the way.'

'Please, Titus,' Hazel said. 'Bramley's keen – aren't you?'

'Oh, yes,' the dormouse replied flatly. 'Very keen.'

'I'm worried that the Witch Hunters will notice him,' Hazel said. 'And I just think that while I'm in the Tower it'll be safer for both of us if I'm on my own.'

Titus ruminated for a while, then held out his hand. 'Very well. Come along, Master Mouse.'

'But where am I to sleep?' Bramley wailed. 'Your hair is so dirty!'

'Oh for God's sake . . .' Titus rummaged in his shirt top pocket and removed several musket balls, some loose tobacco leaves and his spare pipe. 'There, you can move in here.'

Hazel dropped her dejected little familiar inside and stepped away, feeling a tug on her heart. *It's the right thing to do*, she reassured herself. *I'll feel better knowing they're looking out for each other.*

'Well,' she said, suddenly awkward. 'I'd better get going, I suppose.'

Bramley popped his head out of Titus's pocket. 'You need to eat some breakfast.'

'I'll get something on the way.'

'And remember to go out the back door,' Titus said. 'If Treacher sees you in your uniform . . .'

'I know, I know,' Hazel replied. 'Good luck, and *be careful.*'

Titus brushed his hand against her shoulder. 'That goes tenfold for you.'

'Come back soon,' Bramley added.

He looked so forlorn with his whiskers all droopy that Hazel had to force herself not to take him back. 'Just look after each other, will you?' she pleaded, and then left, closing the door behind her.

23
HAZEL PLAYS HER HAND

'They call me the Wandering Scholar.
In truth I flee the demonic servants of Baal.'

Lars Göran Petrov

Hazel was acutely aware of Bramley's absence as she crossed London Bridge; she felt incomplete, impaired, like a puppet with one string cut. Yet she felt freer knowing he was safe from discovery, and she was comforted that he and Titus were together. They would bicker and argue, of course, but they'd look out for each other too.

I just hope they track down the demon before it strikes again, she thought as she sped along the embankment, past the row of ships and round the bend in the river. The White Tower and Cromwell Island loomed into view: two hateful, terrifying twins of stone.

If Murrell would only tell Thorn what I need to know I wouldn't have to go back in and risk my neck again, Hazel thought angrily. *Why is he being so difficult?* She picked up the pace, striding past the guards at the gate and into the Tower precinct. *Because he can, that's why. He's got nothing to lose, and he wants to bargain with me, face to face.*

A guard in the White Tower told her that Hopkins was in the armoury, so she followed him down a set of winding steps into a subterranean chamber. The walls were lined with racks of swords, billhooks, pikes and pistols, and a tang of metal hung in the air.

The soldier pointed to a door leading off from the main room. His hushed voice echoed around the whitewashed walls. 'The General is yonder, in one of his reflective moods.'

Hazel nodded her thanks, wondering if a reflective Hopkins was to her advantage or not, because she had gathered a semblance of an idea on how she might, maybe, *possibly*, get him to do what she wanted.

After straightening her uniform, she marched through the door. The weapons here looked older, obsolete: matchlocks with ornate firing mechanisms, swords even taller than she was, and medieval halberds stacked together like sheaves of wheat. Lamplight flickered off a line of battered breastplates hanging from the wall.

She found Hopkins at the far end of the room, looking at a magnificent suit of armour. 'Apprentice Lowe reporting for duty, General,' she said, standing to attention.

'With hammer and heat a man may bend steel into such grand things as this.' Hopkins turned to her with a wry smile. 'If only people were so . . . *malleable*.'

'So Murrell still has not spoken up?'

Hopkins shook his head.

'I'm sure the Oven will take its toll soon,' Hazel said, seeing an opportunity to steer the conversation in the direction she required. 'Actually, General, I wanted—'

'This was King Henry the Eighth's armour,' Hopkins said. 'The last of England's great kings, before his daughter, Elizabeth, ushered in a new age of so-called tolerance.' He spat the last word out like poison. 'Did you know that Henry had two of his wives beheaded for witchcraft? Some say the old King was hounded to his grave by their vengeful ghosts.'

And what about you, General? Hazel thought bitterly. *Do the ghosts of those you've killed haunt your dreams?*

'Does our work today involve Nicolas Murrell, General?' she asked.

'Of course it does. Time is pressing now the date of his execution is set.' Hopkins ran his thumb over the blade of a battleaxe, then began to pace around the chamber. 'We've been getting a lot of valuable information from a young lad Murrell held captive for a while.'

He means David, Hazel thought.

'And this lad has told us that Murrell had been treating with a demon prince called Baal,' Hopkins continued with a shake of his head. 'He opened a portal between our world and that of the demons. We in the Order knew Murrell was dangerous, but to carry out such a reckless act – the hubris of it takes my breath away.'

Hazel knew all this. Indeed, she had witnessed Murrell open the howling, seething gateway into the Underworld, and watched helpless as the demon Baal had snatched her mother and dragged her down into the depths of his domain.

These memories haunted her every waking moment, and her every troubled sleep.

She affected a look of horror. 'How awful that a man would do such a thing. What was Murrell bargaining with this . . . *Baal* . . . for?'

'The boy, David, doesn't remember. It seems he was bitten by one of Murrell's demonic familiars, and the poison administered is affecting his memory. My best apothecaries are trying to cure him but they say there is little hope. They know nothing of demon poisons.'

Hazel swallowed. So David was still suffering from the spider-demon Spindle's poison. And if it was eroding his memories, what would it cause next? Madness? *Death?* Guilt gnawed at her. *If I can get Ma back, she might be able to cure him.*

Their circuit of the chamber had brought them back to King Henry's armour. 'I *must* find out what Murrell's bargain was,' Hopkins murmured, looking up at the grilled visor. 'What promises were made? What unholy bargains struck?'

'So what are you going to do?'

'I've had him brought out of the Oven for another interrogation that I shall lead. I can only hope the heat and discomfort have softened him up enough to talk, but I'm not too optimistic about that.' Hopkins took a curved blade from his pocket and held it up to the light. 'If only there was a way I could open up his skull, poke into his brains and expose his thoughts to the light.'

Hazel decided now was the time to test the waters. 'General, may I speak plainly on this matter of Murrell, and his stubborn refusal to talk?'

Hopkins sat on a bench by the wall and began to scrape his blade under each already spotless fingernail. 'You may.'

'My father says that madness is doing the same thing again and again and expecting different results.'

Hopkins frowned at her. 'That sounds like impertinence, William.'

'My apologies, General,' Hazel said, with a deferential bow. 'What I mean is that you've been administering to Murrell personally, haven't you? With your clerks and scribes present to record his every word?'

'I have. He's an important prisoner.'

'Exactly!' Hazel snapped her fingers. 'And he knows his importance and the information he withholds from you is what keeps him alive.'

'I suppose so,' Hopkins said slowly. 'What of it?'

Hazel leaned towards the General, close enough to see a raw-pink rash spreading under his collar. 'So what if we made him feel *less* important? Give him the impression that you had better things to do than talk to him?'

'It would certainly hurt his twisted sense of pride,' Hopkins said, running a hand down his chin.

'And perhaps be enough to coax him into giving up some information to regain your interest.'

'Mmm, I remain to be convinced . . .'

Hazel felt her chance slipping away. She spoke quickly

and urgently. 'If you can get Murrell to open up even a fraction, to give you any hint of his plans or knowledge about Baal, it might be enough for you to argue your case to Lord Cromwell about keeping him alive a while longer to find out more.'

'Yes, perhaps . . .' A slow smile spread over Hopkins' round face. 'And that would certainly stick in Stearne's craw.'

'Oh, he'll be *livid*,' Hazel said, daring to feel a flash of hope. 'I know it's a long shot, but so far none of your efforts have got him to talk. So this has got to be worth a try, don't you think?'

Hopkins sat in the shadow of the King's armour, twirling his blade between his fingers. 'Very well. You can speak to him, but not for long. He's a dangerous man.'

24
HOPKINS' BROTHER

One witch can be made to give up another,
and she another, and she yet another.
A Forest of Gallows by Albrecht Prinz

'Is this really necessary?' Bramley squeaked from Titus's top pocket. 'Surely there's some other way?'

'Not that I can think of,' Titus said, striding down a road of mean dwellings on the outskirts of Southwark. 'We know the killer is wearing a plague doctor's uniform, so the next stage of our investigation naturally leads us to their Guild. I want a good root about. See what's what.'

'But why the deception? Can't you just go in and ask your questions?'

'Of course not! The Guild of Plague Doctors is notoriously secretive – they're not going to give information to just anybody. So I need to spin them a lie.'

'But they won't believe you,' Bramley said, whiskers quivering with fear. 'Posing as Hopkins' brother? We don't even know if he *has* a brother!'

'That doesn't matter a jot. The bigger the lie the more likely people are to buy it – as long as you sell it with utter and complete conviction.' He slowed down as they reached the end of the road. 'There it is: the Guildhall of the Plague Doctors.'

Ahead, standing alone in a weed-infested courtyard, was a large, crooked building of sagging timbers, brown plaster and dirty mullioned windows. A sign in the shape of a beaked mask hung over the door.

'Look familiar?' Titus asked.

'Yes,' Bramley whispered. 'That's what the demon wore over its head.'

'Good. Then we're on the right track.' Titus pushed Bramley down into this pocket. 'Come along then, Master Mouse, let us consort with the plague doctors.' He strode up to the door and threw it open without knocking.

Inside was a small, shabby reception room with several doors and a rickety staircase leading up to the next floor. Two men stood in the corner. One, red-faced and sweating, was in the process of removing his leather plague-doctor robe. His beaked mask lay flattened on the table beside him. The other wore a rather unkempt periwig and a faded yellow frock coat. Both men stopped talking, outraged at the interruption.

Undeterred, Titus addressed the periwigged man. 'Are you the Guild Master?'

'I am,' the man replied, puffing up indignantly. 'And who are you to barge into my Hall—?'

'You should know who I am,' Titus growled. 'Indeed, you should be expecting my visit. I had my office send a missive to you last week.'

'Missive? I don't recall . . .' The Guild Master rallied himself. 'Look here, my man, just who the devil are you?'

Titus stood up straight, his impressive six-foot-four-inches towering over the Guild Master. 'I am Lord Frederick Hopkins. Brother and confidant of the Witch Hunter General himself, and I come this day from the *Tower*.'

The effect of this statement was dramatic and immediate. The Guild Master paled. 'H-Hopkins' brother?' he said.

The other man, now free of his robe, muttered 'Excuse me, sirs' and scurried up the stairs.

Titus glowered. 'Are you not in the habit of reading your missives?'

'I'm sure I would have remembered . . .' he replied, quaking like gelatine. 'Perhaps we should discuss this in my office, Lord Hopkins?'

'Very well,' Titus said, feeling the warmth of Bramley giving out a pulse of admiring magic.

The Guild Master showed him into a poky room lined with black ledgers, each marked with a month and a year: the *Books of the Dead* as recorded by the Plague Doctors through the decades. Titus swept past, sat down behind the desk and said nothing, leaving the Guild Master standing helplessly adrift on the other side.

'Your honourable missive, your illustrious visit,' he gabbled. 'To what does it relate?'

'Troubling rumours about your Guild, the conduct of your men, and *you*.' Titus took off his hat, keeping his glare fixed on the Guild Master. 'Black magic. *Witchcraft*.'

The Guild Master looked about ready to faint. 'W–witchcraft?' he said, his voice barely audible. 'I don't under—'

'Death on your streets, this month just passed. Murder!' Titus stood up and slammed a fist on to the desk, causing the Guild Master to utter a little cry. 'Young children found with their faces contorted with fear. Have you heard about this?'

'Yes, but I took it to be idle gossip . . . superstitious nonsense . . .'

Titus shook his head. 'Not so. I have seen the bodies, and the marks left on them point to sorcery of the foulest kind.'

'B-but even if that's the case, begging your pardon, what has it to do with me?'

'Because there was a witness to the latest deadly deed –' Titus paused for effect – 'and he says the perpetrator wore the uniform . . . of a plague doctor.'

The Guild Master collapsed on to a chair by the wall, gasping, his pallor turning green.

'The witness was most adamant in his recollections,' Titus continued mercilessly, 'and the evidence suggests that the killer resides in your Guild.'

'No, no . . . None of my men, I swear . . .'

'I have the authority *and* the inclination to throw every man-jack of you at the mercy of the interrogators – they'll loosen a few tongues.' Titus strode to the door and then paused. 'Unless you can furnish me with information to point me in a more focused direction? Think hard,

137

Guild Master, and do not lie.'

The Guild Master ran a handkerchief over his greasy brow, his eyes roving feverishly around the room as if seeking an answer written on the walls. 'Wait!' he cried. 'One of my men has not reported to work for weeks. No one's seen hide nor hair of him.'

'Since when?'

'Three weeks, a month perhaps.'

'So just before the killings began.' Titus narrowed his eyes. 'This man – was he especially tall?'

'Yes, *yes*! Abnormally so.'

'And he wore the uniform – robe, beaked mask?'

The Guild Master nodded.

'You've earned yourself a reprieve,' Titus said. 'Now give me his name and address, quickly now. And do not mention this to anyone. If you do, I'll come back here with my brother.'

25
A HARD WON MEETING

The Underworld rings with a constant
symphony of destruction.
The Five Magics by Nikolas Menza

'I'm having second thoughts about this,' Hopkins said.

Hazel and the Witch Hunter General stood outside the same cell they had spoken to Murrell in before.

'I understand you're worried about me,' Hazel said. 'But sending a mere apprentice like me in to talk to Murrell is the best way to make him think he's no longer important to you.'

Hopkins shook his head. 'He's a dangerous man, and you're just a child . . .'

'I'm the son of a rat-catcher, and I've dealt with vermin like him my whole life.' She looked Hopkins in the eye. 'Please, General, let me prove myself.'

Hazel stopped herself from flinching when Hopkins rested a soft hand on her shoulder and leaned closer. 'Don't stay in there long. Just needle his pride by making him think I've got something better to do than talk to him.'

Wrestling with the fact that a man as cruel as Hopkins

139

actually cared about her, Hazel said, 'I understand, General. I'll be careful.'

Hopkins stepped to one side. The guard opened the door and Hazel marched in. The door clanged shut behind her, blocking all sound from outside. She shivered. The stone walls swallowed the lantern light and gave nothing but damp in return.

No chair for Murrell this time; strung up by his wrists with a rope running through a loop in the ceiling, and with barely enough slack to allow his toes to touch the floor, he slowly raised his head and regarded Hazel with sunken, pain-filled eyes. He looked much worse than before, and Hazel felt a rush of pity.

'Well well,' he said in a voice as cracked as old china. 'Hazel Hooper. In what guise are you visiting me today? As witch, or Witch Hunter?'

'As a witch, of course!' Hazel hissed. 'All this –' she tugged on her uniform – 'is so I can talk to you about Ma, and how you're going to help me get her back.'

Murrell smiled. 'If I still had my hat, I would tip it to you. It seems your resourcefulness knows no bounds.'

Hazel hurried over to where the rope was secured to the wall. 'I'm going to loosen this so you can stand properly.' Murrell groaned as she let out some slack and then retied the knot. 'Better?'

'Yes. Thank you.' He swivelled round to face her. 'How did you arrange to speak to me alone like this?'

'I convinced Hopkins that making you feel less important

might loosen your tongue,' Hazel said, circling the cell.

'Clever girl. You can come closer, you know. I won't bite. After all, you're the only friend I have in this hellhole.'

'We're not friends,' Hazel said coldly. But she sidled towards him regardless, taking a flask from her pocket and giving him a few mouthfuls of small beer.

'Ally, then,' Murrell replied, licking the last drops of liquid from his parched lips. 'Old adversaries forced to work together, yes? Help each other out?'

'The only help I can give you is by allowing you to do the right thing by my mother,' Hazel said. 'Now tell me how I can get to her. Quickly – Hopkins might come at any moment . . .'

'Thorn told me that's what you wanted, but I'd already guessed when your mouse came to see me.' His voice became more urgent. 'Listen, Hazel, you can't just recite a few magic words and simply stroll into the heart of the demon world.'

'I know that,' Hazel said, casting a nervous glance towards the door. 'I've been reading all Titus's books—'

'Reading a book is not the same as understanding it,' Murrell interrupted. 'You're not a scholar, you're a child who's spent most of her life closeted away in the forest. You don't have any idea of the dangers you'll be dealing with. But I do.' He shook his chains. 'Get me out of this place and I'll open the demon gate for you *and* I'll accompany you into the Underworld – it's your best hope of getting your mother back safely.'

141

Hazel's skin glowed with an angry flush of magic. 'And what of the walls, the gates, the guards?' she said, her voice shaking with frustration. 'I can't help you escape, Murrell, you know that.'

'I think a witch who can infiltrate the Order can do anything she turns her mind to. I don't want to die in here, Hazel. I promise to help if only you would *set me free!*'

For the first time Hazel saw fear in his eyes, and she realized that if she could, if there was even the slimmest hope of success, she would try to save him from the terrible fate she knew awaited him at the hands of the Order. But there wasn't. It was impossible.

'I cannot,' she said, looking away to hide her shame.

Murrell sagged in his chains. 'Then go.'

'Please, Nicolas, do the right thing. Not for me, but my mother. You still care about her, don't you?'

'Sending you alone into the Underworld after her is a death sentence – how can I add that to my already troubled conscience? Don't you see? Everything I touch falls into ruins. My plans, my Coven, all gone.'

'But I'm offering you a chance to right one of your wrongs.'

The chain rattled as Murrell leaned closer. 'You have got to learn that life is cruel. It takes, and it destroys, and there is nothing we – we who are but *ants* – can do about it.'

Hazel spoke quietly, determinedly. 'I don't care. I love my ma and I know she'd do the same for me. I'm going to find a way to her with or without you, Nicolas Murrell.' She turned to leave, already thinking about what she was going to do next.

'Wait,' Murrell said dully. 'If you really want to do this, I'll help you on your way. But be warned, I cannot protect you from the demons you will face if you leave me in this prison.'

Hazel turned round. 'I just want to know how to open the gate. I'll figure out how to survive on the other side of it myself.'

'Very well,' Murrell sighed. 'You're going to need a rare book and some demon blood with which to draw a very particular magic circle . . .'

26
ONE WAY OUT

Ten minutes later, and armed with the information she needed, Hazel knocked on the door for the guard to let her out. She had decided not to tell Murrell about his impending execution. What would be the point? It would only compound his misery, and make his last few days more miserable.

If I could help him escape I would, but it's impossible.

The door opened and without a backwards glance Hazel walked out, looking as calm as her jangling nerves allowed.

'The General awaits you on the ground floor, Master Apprentice,' the guard said.

Hazel thought he sounded nervous, and as she hurried down the steps the idea was confirmed by what was occurring below: guards herded prisoners back to their cells, orders were shouted, doors slammed, bolts driven home – the previous atmosphere of grim oppression had transformed into one of frenzied activity.

An acid bubble of fear seared Hazel's throat. Was this

about her? Had they discovered that she was a witch?

Hopkins stood by the main door, deep in conversation with Grimstone and the Spymaster. Grimstone was speaking quickly and urgently, while the Spymaster listened, hunched over his walking stick like an ancient crow.

Hazel flinched as Hopkins glanced up and saw her. He snapped his fingers and beckoned. Fighting her fear, she hurried down the steps on legs so wobbly she thought she might fall.

'Are you certain, Spymaster?' Hopkins was saying as Hazel joined them. 'Cromwell's been missing for *two days*?'

'The dispatch rider arrived from Harrogate this very hour with the news,' the Spymaster replied gravely. 'Cromwell's deputy, General Fleetwood, is in charge but you can imagine the disarray up there.'

'Good God,' Hopkins breathed.

Hazel listened attentively, greatly relieved that the activity had nothing to do with her. *Will the rebels in the North be able to take advantage of Cromwell's disappearance?* she thought. *And what does it mean for Hopkins?*

'Is the news widely known?' Grimstone asked.

'Not yet, but it will be,' the Spymaster said.

'Bad news runs fastest.' Hopkins rubbed a finger under his collar, and Hazel saw a nervous rash spreading up to his ears.

She hid a grim smile; it was good to see Hopkins squirm, and all this confusion meant she might have a better chance of escaping. *Just need to pick my moment and slip away.*

'I've put the garrison on high alert,' Grimstone said, 'and doubled the guard at the gates.'

Hopkins nodded, deep in thought. 'Cromwell, missing... What happened?'

The Spymaster shrugged. 'No one knows for sure. He was reconnoitring with a squadron of his Ironsides and never returned. The best hope is he's lost in enemy territory.'

'The worst scenario is he's fallen into the rebels' clutches, or he's dead,' Grimstone said.

'God's bones,' Hopkins said. 'He's at war – why doesn't he stay in the command tent like most generals?'

The Spymaster pressed a long-nailed finger into Hopkins' chest. 'The point is, Matthew, with Cromwell missing, *you* are in charge and must be safeguarded from all possible danger, whether it comes from without . . . or within.'

Hopkins and the Grandees headed towards the gate as a troop of soldiers marched past in double-time. Hazel followed, trying to hear their conversation over the tramp of boots.

'Any rebel spies will be emboldened by this news,' Grimstone said, 'and they might even try to land a blow against us. Against *you*, General.'

'That is true. Suggestions?'

Hazel saw a chance to perhaps give Murrell a stay of execution. She raised her hand. 'Sirs?' Surprised, the three men stopped and turned to her. 'I couldn't help but overhear your troubling news, and I wonder if perhaps you should postpone the Execution Pageant.'

The Spymaster looked flabbergasted at her interruption. '*What?*'

'If the wretched rebels were to take advantage of the present circumstances,' Hazel said, ignoring his hostility, 'would the Execution Pageant not be the perfect time to strike against the Order?'

Hopkins raised his eyebrow and gave her a fleeting look of approval. 'Perhaps we should consider—'

'Absolutely not,' the Spymaster interrupted. 'The preparations have already begun and the announcements have been made. If we cancel the Pageant it will be seen as a sign of weakness. Do you agree, Grimstone?'

Hazel was disappointed when Grimstone nodded. 'We must continue as if nothing is amiss, General.'

'And in the meantime we need to vet everyone who has joined the Order in the past few weeks,' the Spymaster said without taking his gimlet eye from Hazel. 'Starting with your impertinent new apprentice. I don't like the look of him.'

'I'll round up all the new recruits and keep them locked up, then send my interrogators to check the local records, verify family details, that sort of thing,' Grimstone said with a sigh.

Cold fingers of panic gripped Hazel's heart. Even a cursory check of the personal details she had given during her induction interview would reveal her web of lies – she had to get out of here, right now.

'Such precautions should be a matter of course,' the

Spymaster grumbled as they emerged on to the bridge. 'Things have got too lax around here.'

Grimstone shot him a poisonous glance.

'Very well, but be as quick as you can,' Hopkins said. 'I need William by my side, especially now.'

Hazel trailed after them into the dazzling sunshine. Her feet felt encased in lead, her insides hollow.

The interrogators won't find any record of Saxondale and Lowe's Rat-Catchers in Putney, or a William Lowe. Then they'll interrogate me, examine me, find out I'm a girl . . . find out I'm a witch . . .

The bridge and embankment teemed with soldiers and Witch Hunters on high alert; Hazel would not be able to slip or run away through them all unnoticed. She could use fire-magic to fight her way out, but that would mean hurting or even killing people.

No, I've got to think of some other way. Hazel glanced over the side of the bridge at the grey water sliding past. The railing was low – easy to climb.

I could jump in and swim for shore, she thought. *But if I do that, Hopkins will know I've been up to something, and he and his cronies will turn London upside down looking for me.*

They were nearly halfway across the bridge. Gulls taunted Hazel overhead. Downstream an East India trade ship slipped her moorings and began its ponderous turn into the tide.

She had to get away but also convince Hopkins it was

for a reason other than escape. But how? It was almost impossible to think straight with the prospect of discovery hanging over her head.

Hopkins dropped back a pace to talk to her. 'Well, William? How went it with Murrell?'

An idea occurred at the mention of the demonologist's name: it was perfect, it was *brilliant*, but she knew that Murrell would pay a high price if she put it into action.

I'm sorry, Nicolas, but this is the only way.

'Murrell,' Hazel said in a croaky voice. 'Murrell, Murrell . . .'

'William?' Hopkins said. 'What on earth's the matter?'

He jumped as Hazel let out a cry and gripped her head in both hands. 'My mind . . . it burns with his thoughts . . . He spoke to me, but he did not move his lips . . .'

Hopkins took a step towards her. 'What's wrong? Tell me!'

'His words are in my head,' Hazel cried, staring imploringly at Hopkins. 'Get them out!'

'The boy speaks in riddles,' the Spymaster snapped, waving his walking stick at her. 'Stop it at once!'

'I fear sorcery,' Grimstone hissed. '*Possession!*'

Hazel tugged her hair and dragged her nails over her face. 'Get them *out*! Get them *out*!' she screamed, backing ever closer to the rail.

Grimstone looked terrified; even the old Spymaster seemed disturbed. Nearby guards turned to see what the commotion was.

Hopkins approached her, reaching out with one hand. 'William Lowe,' he said. 'Look at me, lad. Don't be afraid ...'

Hazel went rigid and rolled her eyes back so only the whites showed.

Hopkins stopped, looking uncertain for the first time. 'I knew I shouldn't have let you in there alone.'

'I have ... a message ... for the Burner of Witches,' Hazel said in a shrill, toneless voice.

'I don't want your message,' Hopkins said. 'I want Junior Apprentice William Lowe back.'

Hazel cocked her head to one side. 'The message is: *I win.*' And before the horrified Hopkins could grab her, she stepped on to the parapet, spread her arms and plummeted into the river.

27
HOUSE OF THE PLAGUE DOCTOR

Board up the House.
Hide your boys and girls!
Plague Songs by John Dyler Baizley

According to the Guild Master, the missing plague doctor's name was Peter Feldspar, and he lived alone on Butchers Lane in Southwark.

Titus, with Bramley peeping out of his top pocket, stared at the house from the other side of the street. Both wore worried frowns.

'The Guild Master didn't say that Feldspar had the plague,' Titus said out of the corner of his mouth.

'Then why is there a big red cross on his front door?' Bramley replied. 'Are you sure this is the right house?'

'Pretty sure. And if Feldspar does have the plague and has been shut in all this time, that would explain his absence from work.'

'He might be dead,' Bramley said, whiskers quivering.

'Or he might just be riddled with sickness. Either way we have to go inside. Feldspar might be our killer. Or someone—'

'Or some*thing* . . .'

'Or some*thing* did away with him and stole his plague-doctor uniform.' Titus checked his pistol was loaded and tucked it into his belt. 'Time to find out.'

'Wait!' Bramley squealed. 'The demon might be in there, at this moment, waiting for us!'

'What a querulous little creature you are. Would you like me to leave you here in the gutter? No? Then come along.'

Titus looked up and down the street. The houses were sad, tumbledown affairs, and most of the residents were either at work or attending the decrepit market at the far end. The windows of Feldspar's house were shuttered, but to Titus's surprise the front door was unlocked. It creaked as he pushed it open.

Stung by Titus's taunts, Bramley scrambled up the old Witch Finder's arm and perched bravely on his shoulder. 'Careful,' he whispered. 'Don't make any noise.'

'You're the one making all the noise.' When Titus took his hand from the door the tips of his fingers were covered in dry red flakes. He sniffed the substance. His heart beat faster.

'Mouse,' he whispered, taking the pistol from his belt. 'That plague cross on the door – it's been drawn with blood.'

'Blood?' Bramley replied. 'Don't they usually use paint?'

'Of course they do . . . Something is amiss.'

Putting aside all thoughts of personal hygiene, Bramley hid himself in Titus's hair.

Titus stepped inside the house and closed the door. Now

the only light came from the cracks around the shutters, but it was enough to see a comfortably furnished sitting room, a kitchen leading off at the back, and a flight of stairs to the first floor.

The house appeared deserted, but both Titus and Bramley felt uneasy. Moving quietly for a big man, Titus climbed the stairs to find a small bedroom. Fragrant rushes covered the floor, and the bed was neatly made.

'A tidy cove,' he muttered.

'Yes, but where *is* he?'

Titus opened the wardrobe and found several jackets, coats and shirts hanging on a rail. He sniffed. 'Leather and herbs. That's what I'd expect a plague doctor's robe to smell of, but there's no sign of it here.'

'Why herbs?' Bramley said, risking an excursion back on to Titus's shoulder.

'That's what the beaks on the masks are for – for filling with herbs which are believed to ward off plaguey vapours.'

Titus went to the window and looked down on to a small garden, fenced on all sides and flourishing with potatoes and string beans. What he saw in the far corner made his heart sink. 'I think I know where our Mr Feldspar is,' he said, heading back downstairs.

He stopped on the threshold to the kitchen and found it in disarray. The chair lay smashed in the corner, and the floor was covered in broken crockery and glass. A pan of stew, crawling with maggots, stood on a stone-cold stove.

'A struggle took place here,' Bramley said.

'Aye, a mortal one. And it happened a few weeks ago, judging by that rancid food.'

'So we think the killer stalked Feldspar back to his house, murdered him as he prepared his supper and stole his robes to use as a disguise?' Bramley said, stroking his whiskers thoughtfully.

'I'll make a detective of you yet, Master Mouse. I also think the killer used poor Feldspar's blood for the plague cross on the door – what better way to ensure no one discovers the crime?' Titus frowned and picked up a carving knife from the floor. He ran his finger over the blade and it came away covered in a sticky white residue. 'Well, well – it seems Feldspar didn't go down without a fight. Look here, this is demon blood.'

Bramley sniffed and wrinkled his nose. 'Sour milk.'

'So you were right,' Titus murmured, his eyes straying to the back door. 'You, Hazel, Old Seb . . . It *is* a demon we hunt. And it was in this very room.'

From his pocket he retrieved a brass tube about the length of a man's thumb. The middle comprised of a set of parallel dials covered with tiny etched writing, and there was a copper eyepiece and a smooth glass lens at each end.

'If I knew what demon we were dealing with I could set this Entropy Monocle to pick up its tracks and we could follow it to its lair,' Titus said. 'But without that knowledge . . . I fear the trail has already gone cold.'

'How can we find out what sort of demon it is?' Bramley said, climbing back down into Titus's top pocket.

'I don't know . . . yet. I need to do some research using what we do know about this beast – it's back to the wagon after this so I can get my books.' He headed into the garden and stopped by the pile of freshly dug earth that he'd seen from the bedroom window.

'What's under there?' Bramley asked.

'The last piece of the puzzle,' Titus said. The fence around the garden was high – no one would see what he was about to do. 'I'm going to need a spade.'

28
PLOTS AND PLANS

*'The rebels inhabit the northern counties, striking
our encampments and disappearing into the night.'*
Lord Protector Oliver Cromwell, on campaign

It was early evening when Hazel trudged back to the tavern, and the sun had mostly dried her hair and uniform. She sneaked up to the balcony and through the back door, relieved to find the corridor deserted. Laughter and the hum of conversation drifted up from the taproom.

The fire in her room was already laid with kindling so Hazel lit it with a deft flick of magic. Then she laid out her uniform and the official Order seal to dry, just in case she needed them again. Another flick of magic heated the water in the washbasin, and after scrubbing the worst of the river off her skin she got dressed.

It felt good to be back in her old clothes: the faded but oh-so-comfortable dress, her woollen stockings and lace-up leather boots. *I feel more like myself again*, she thought, enjoying the warmth of the fire. *Goodbye, Apprentice Lowe. Hello, Hazel Hooper.*

The tang of the Thames still clung to her hair. She remembered the terrifying lack of control as the river had grabbed and swept her under the bridge, and how just when she thought her lungs would pop, she had surfaced, gasping for air, but free.

And now here I am, back at the tavern. I wonder how Titus and Bram fared?

She found the old Witch Finder at the table in his room, poring over a leather-bound edition of *Demonology*. 'Good evening, *Father*,' she said, doffing an imaginary hat. 'Your dutiful daughter Lizzie is back from catching rats.'

A brief smile appeared beneath Titus's beard. 'Back at last,' he said. 'About time. Now you can relieve me of your troublesome rodent.'

Hazel skipped to the desk. 'Where *is* the little tyke?'

Titus nodded to where Bramley lay curled up asleep in his upturned palm. 'I haven't been able to move for two hours,' he grumbled.

'Why not?' Hazel laughed. 'I would have!'

'It just seemed a shame to disturb him . . .'

'I think you two have become *friends*,' Hazel teased.

Bramley stirred, opened one eye, and leaped up. 'Hazel!' he cried, then scampered up her arm and dived headfirst into her hair. He quickly re-emerged with a wrinkled nose. 'Urgh! It smells terrible in there. What *have* you been up to?'

'Yes, let's hear it,' Titus said, flexing his fingers. 'I take it from your cheerful demeanour that you were successful?'

And so, after Titus had brought up drinks and supper from the kitchen, Hazel told them everything that had befallen her. She related the events quietly, sitting on the bed with her hands clasped in her lap, with her companions listening in increasing amazement.

'So you pretended to be bewitched by Murrell and jumped into the river?' Bramley said from his perch on top of Titus's empty ale mug. 'But you could have *drowned*!'

Hazel shrugged. 'I had to. It was the only way to get away before Hopkins locked me up and checked my story.'

Titus tamped some tobacco into his pipe, then passed it to Hazel. She obliged him with a spark of magic and gave the smoking pipe back. 'In all my long years I don't think I have ever met anyone like you,' he said.

'*Thank* you, Titus.'

'Stubborn, wilful, deceitful,' Titus continued, puffing on his pipe, 'and reckless to the point of stupidity.'

Hazel's smile faded. 'I thought you were paying me a compliment.'

Titus's eyes widened. 'Oh, but I am.'

'I'd have added "pig-headed" to the list,' Bramley said, scampering up her arm and giving her an affectionate nip on the ear.

'So,' Titus said, 'Murrell said you need a book to open the demon gate. What book?'

'He said it was called the, er, *Nec-ron-om-icon*. *Necronomicon* – yes, that was it. He said you'd know all about it.'

'The *Necronomicon*,' Titus murmured, leaning back in his chair. 'Oh, I've heard of it, all right. It's infamous for containing forbidden knowledge about all things demonic. How did Murrell get hold of it?'

'He told me he stole it from the Forbidden Library in a place called Constantinople. There was only ever one copy, so he took that one.'

'He stole it from the Ottoman Sultan?' Titus chuckled. 'Murrell's got gumption, I'll give him that.'

'Did he have it at his hideout in Rivenpike?' Bramley asked. 'Is that where we have to go next?'

Hazel shook her head. 'No, the Witch Hunters took it after they arrested him. So the question is: where are they keeping it?'

'My best guess would be the Great Library in Baynards Castle. It used to be the Witch Finders' London headquarters, and where we stored all our dangerous grimoires. If the Order have the *Necronomicon*, that's where they'd keep it.'

'So I need to get inside. But how?'

'Same as before, I think,' Titus said. 'Sneaky infiltration. Do you still have your uniform?'

'It's drying in the other room,' Hazel sighed. 'I can't believe I'm having to tangle with the Order again.'

A smile split Titus's craggy face. 'Cheer up, slop-sprite,' he said. 'It won't be so bad.'

'Why not?'

'Because this time I'm coming with you.'

29
AN ESTEEMED PRUSSIAN VISITOR

'People can lose their lives in libraries.
They ought to be warned.'
Mr S. Bellow, Halifax Library Custodian

The trio decided that if they were to retrieve the *Necronomicon* they might as well do so that night. According to Titus, Baynards Castle was a formidable fortress – not the sort of place you could sneak into unnoticed. So they agreed on a ruse and went their separate ways to prepare.

Hazel quickly changed back into her dried-out apprentice's uniform and put Bramley on her shoulder – it felt good to have him back. There was a knock on the door and Titus entered.

'Well?' How do I look?' he said, turning in a slow circle.

Hazel was exhausted, and the thought of once again infiltrating the Order so soon after escaping seemed too much like tempting fate, but the sight of Titus Transformed cheered her up immensely. 'You look . . . extraordinary.'

The old Witch Finder had brushed down his clothes and hat and polished his boots to a decent shine. His hair was washed and tied back with a black ribbon, and his beard was neatly combed. A monocle twinkled in his eye and his waist was girdled with a wide red sash.

'Really very smart,' Bramley added approvingly. 'And *clean*.'

Titus clicked his heels together. 'Baron Karl von Hake, envoy from the Prussian League Against Witches, at your service,' he said, affecting a thick Germanic accent.

'Huh. Quite the actor, aren't you?' Bramley said.

'I'm impressed.' Hazel grinned. 'I think we're as ready as we'll ever be. Time to get the book.'

Baynards Castle was a long way westward from London Bridge, so Titus suggested they hire a wherry across the river to save time and a tiring walk. It was Hazel's first time in a boat, and she spent the whole crossing clinging on to the gunwales with both hands and trying to ignore the sickening pitch and roll. Bramley did his best to soothe her by gently stroking her neck with his tail.

Titus conversed cheerfully with the wherryman in his Prussian accent – '*Ja*, London is a glorious city, much admired in my country . . . So many people from all over our globe . . .'

It was a bright, moonlit night. Silver light bathed the rooftops and the smooth river shone like a tarnished mirror. Ahead, and getting closer with each pull of the wherryman's oars, loomed Baynards Castle.

It was an imposing sight: octagonal towers and high walls faced with light grey stone rose from the water, the giant foundation stones encased in layers of green tidal mud. Rows of windows glowed from within, and far above a line of sharply pitched roofs cut into the sky like teeth.

The wherry bumped to a stop at the foot of a flight of steps leading up to the castle door. After telling the wherryman to await their return, Titus and Hazel climbed out, being careful not to slip on the wet stone.

'Remember what I said,' Titus whispered as they mounted the steps. 'Be credible, and above all be confident.'

'I have done this sort of thing before, you know,' Hazel replied.

Two guards in gleaming breastplates watched as they approached the gate.

'*Schnell*, Master Anthony!' Titus said in his Prussian accent. 'Your English food has played havoc with my internals. I find myself in urgent need of the *Badezimmer*.'

The tallest guard had a sergeant's ribbon tied around his arm. 'State your business,' he said, looking at Titus curiously.

'I'm apprenticed to General Hopkins,' Hazel replied, 'here to escort his esteemed guest, Baron von Hake, to the Library.'

The sergeant looked closely at Hazel. 'I've not seen you before, and I know all of the General's apprentices.'

'I was only recruited this week, at Sir Grimstone's behest.'

'*Badezimmer, bitte*,' Titus said plaintively.

'The Baron sampled some pickled eggs and they seem to

have disagreed with him,' Hazel said, giving the sergeant a surreptitious eye-roll. 'Here's the General's seal.'

The sergeant examined it, gave them both another appraising glance, then ushered them into a hall hung with tapestries and mounted deer heads. 'Welcome to Baynards Castle.' He pointed to a set of winding steps. 'Privies are on the first floor, library's at the top.'

'Most obliged,' Hazel said, heading for the steps. 'Follow me, please, Baron.'

They ascended the staircase to the very top and entered a small reception room. A white-haired man sat behind a desk, examining a book so closely his nose almost touched the pages. Hazel coughed politely.

'Mmm? Yes? What is it, girl?' the old man said, squinting at her with pale, watery eyes.

'Girl?' Hazel echoed, feeling Bramley tense up behind her ear.

'*Mädchen?*' Titus said. '*Master Anthony ist kein Mädchen!*'

'My name is Anthony, sir,' Hazel said. 'General Hopkins' apprentice.'

'Ah, so you are, so you are,' the old man said. 'It's just that you have very girlish features, and my eyes are not as sharp as once they were.'

'I'm here at the General's behest,' Hazel said. 'Allow me to introduce Baron Karl von Hake, envoy from our esteemed compatriots the Prussian League Against Witches. I'm here to show him the Great Library.'

The old man un-hunched to his feet and gave a stiff bow. 'Welcome, Baron. I'm the head librarian, Mr Albert Graves. I'm a great admirer of the League. Such zeal! Such efficiency!'

Titus clicked his heels together. '*Danke*, Herr Graves. Your collection here is the envy of Europe. My colleagues in Prussia are ... *eifersüchtig* ... er, *jealous*, that I am to be perusing you.'

'And we are pleased to have you, Baron . . .' Graves paused and looked at Hazel. 'Although it's rather late for a visit, is it not?'

'Ah, with much regret, I am having to cut to size my visit to London with abruptness,' Titus said. 'News from Dietersburg – a witch coven is discovered, and they need my expertise at the, er . . . I seek the word . . . *Hexenprozess* . . . ?' He looked enquiringly at Hazel.

'Witch trial,' she said.

'Witch trial, *ja*. But before I take my leave on the morning sun I desire greatly to look at your *unvergleichliche Bibliothek*.'

Hazel leaned closer to Graves and said quietly, 'The Baron is interested in one book in particular.'

'I'd be happy to oblige, if I can. Which book do mean?'

'A recent acquisition I heard tell you have,' Titus said, 'by that great yet *tragischer* scholar Petrov . . . the dreaded *Necronomicon*.'

'Ah, yes,' Graves nodded. 'We found it in the possession of a particularly dangerous demonologist. We have it safely locked away in our Forbidden Section.'

Titus pressed the palms of his hands together as if in prayer and held them in front of his mouth. 'And may I see this most singular of books, Herr Graves?'

'It would be my pleasure.'

'*Wunderbar, wunderbar!*' Titus said. '*Danke*, Herr Graves.'

Graves smiled and held out his hand. 'If you could just show me your written permission from the General, I'll take you there myself.'

Hazel's face fell. 'Written permission?'

'Naturally,' Graves said. 'I have strict orders not to let anyone, no matter how esteemed –' he gave Titus an ingratiating smile – 'into the Forbidden Section without approval from the General himself.'

'Of course, the paperwork,' Hazel said. 'I have it here somewhere . . .' She patted at her pockets and allowed a look of horror to pass over her face. 'Oh dear, I think I left it back at the Tower . . .'

Titus rounded on her. 'What is this? You don't have the letter from the General? *Dummkopf!*' He turned back to Graves. 'Herr Graves, please do not prohibit me because of the stupidity of this . . . this half— No, this *quarter*-wit!'

Hazel looked humbly at the floor and muttered an apology.

'I'm sorry, Baron,' Graves said. 'But I cannot make an exception.'

'Not even a little peek? *Bitte* . . . *Bitte?*' Titus wheedled.

Graves shook his head. 'I am bound by the rules.'

'I understand, Herr Graves.' Titus grabbed Hazel by the collar. 'Come, *törichter junge*, you can at least show me the *other* books!'

'From whom did you obtain your imps?'
'From Goodwife Brown!'
And like ripples on a pond, the implications spread.
A Forest of Gallows by Albrecht Prinz

Hazel and Titus followed a short corridor into a vast library lit by dozens of lanterns. Books lined the walls from floor to ceiling, with steps on wheels allowing access to the topmost tomes. Long rows of bookcases took up most of the floor space, but there was a reading area where a few men sat in silent study.

Titus breathed deep the smell of leather and parchment. 'I've missed this place,' he said in a reverential tone. 'The wisdom of the world at our fingertips.'

'Yes, very nice,' Bramley whispered. 'Now where's this *Necro*-wotsit?'

'The Forbidden Section used to be over in that corner,' Titus replied. 'Let's take a look.'

Hazel followed him, trailing her fingers over the books and reading the titles embossed on some of the spines: *A View Beyond the Borders of Sanity*; *Hosannas from the Circles of Hell*; *Brann Jente*; *Women in Black*.

'Here we are,' Titus said, keeping his voice low.

Before them stood a wrought-iron gate secured with a chain and three well-oiled padlocks. Beyond was an octagonal room with no other doors or windows – Hazel realized it was situated in one of the castle's corner towers.

Mahogany shelves rose to the ceiling, packed with a multitude of books: leather volumes with embossed spines, books bound with frayed cloth, bundles of parchment tied with twine. One huge volume entitled *Liber Chaotica* had been hinged and bound with bronze. Each book was carefully labelled with its own wooden tag.

In the middle of the room was a plinth, and resting on that plinth was a small and seemingly unremarkable book. The only striking thing about it was the way the cover changed colour depending on what angle it was viewed from: silky green to sapphire blue, tarnished steel to silver. It was both beautiful and unsettling.

'That's it,' Titus said. 'Petrov's *Necronomicon*.'

'The cover,' Hazel breathed. 'All those colours . . .'

'Legend says it's bound in demon skin. Seeing it now I think it's true.'

It looked so close: after all the risk, all the work, success was within Hazel's grasp; she just had to reach out and take it.

'Can you pick those locks?' Bramley asked.

Titus bent down to examine them. 'Probably, but it's going to take time. Time we don't have . . .'

'So what are we going to do?'

Hazel looked around. There was no one nearby and the

bookshelves hid them from view.

'I have an idea,' she said. 'Titus, do you have any string in those deep pockets of yours?'

'Ouch! It's too tight,' Bramley exclaimed as Hazel tied the string around his waist. 'Why is it always me who has to do the dangerous jobs?'

Hazel ignored him and turned to Titus. 'Wait for my signal and then really let rip.'

'Got it,' Titus said as he picked up *The Golden Egg* by Imogen Cooper and made his way back up the aisle towards the reading area.

'Go on, Bram,' Hazel said, putting him down on the other side of the bars. 'It all depends on you now.'

'All right, all right, I'm going . . .'

Holding the other end of the string, Hazel watched her familiar scamper across the floor and scale the lectern, using his claws to dig into the wood. When he reached the top he set to work biting a hole in the corner of the cover. Hazel waited, every passing moment increasing the risk of their discovery.

After he'd finished biting through the leather, Bramley squeezed himself out of the loop of string and threaded it through the hole. Then, taking the loop in his mouth, he clambered down the plinth and back to Hazel.

'Clever mouse,' she breathed, taking his end of the string and letting him climb back on to her shoulder.

Titus was standing ready at the other end of the aisle. On

Hazel's signal he let out a series of racking coughs. Hazel tugged the string and the *Necronomicon* fell to the floor; Titus's outburst covered up the noise of the impact and the scraping sound as she pulled it towards her and picked it up.

The book was small enough to hold in one hand, but it was heavy, as if the words inside held their own terrible weight. The shimmering cover felt dry, and was made up of tiny interlocking scales. *So it is* demon skin. Swallowing her distaste, Hazel tucked it into the back of her trousers and covered it with her jacket.

'We've done it!' Bramley whispered. 'Now we just need to get away.'

Trying to walk as casually as she could, Hazel joined Titus, and together they made their way back to the reception room. They were in luck: Graves had fallen asleep face down on the book he was reading. Down the stairs they went, smelling victory, tasting escape, and into the hall. Ahead was the exit and the wherry waiting for them at the bottom of the stairs.

Hazel saw someone in a fur-lined cloak talking to the guards at the door. She froze and grabbed Titus's arm. 'Grimstone,' she hissed. 'Damn it all, it's *Grimstone*!'

31
...AND OUT THE OTHER

The hearts of men can rise up to the stars,
or sink down to the sewer.
A View from the Boundary by Henri Blofeld

'He's one the Grandees,' Hazel hissed, drawing Titus away from the door. 'He knows me, and what's more, he saw me jump into the river only a few hours ago.'

'Then we need to find another way out of here,' Titus said, his voice tight.

'You know this place best,' Bramley said. 'Any ideas?'

'As a matter of fact I do. And one thing's for certain, Master Mouse, you are going to *hate* it.'

Titus led them back up the stairs and into a small room with rushes on the floor. A bench with six evenly spaced holes cut into the wood ran the length of the wall.

'What *is* this place?' Bramley asked from Hazel's shoulder.

'This,' Titus said, spreading his arms, 'is the room of easement.'

'The room of easement? Funny name ...' Bramley sniffed. 'It has a displeasing odour.'

'Better get used to it.' Titus lifted up the bench and pointed at a sloping stone chute disappearing into murky

171

and odorous darkness. 'Because this is our escape route.'

'The sewer?' Hazel said faintly, peering into the stygian depths. 'Really? I think I'll take my chances with Grimstone . . .'

'Follow me,' Titus said with a geniality that belied the one-way trip into excrement he was about to undertake. 'And try not to be sick, Hazel. You don't want to make the smell any worse.' And with that, he stepped into the bench, crouched with his coat-tails tucked behind his knees, and slid into the darkness with a wet scraping sound.

Hazel knew she had no choice, so with the trepidation of a condemned criminal approaching the chopping block, she also stepped into the latrine. Matter squelched under her boots as she crouched down.

Titus's voice echoed up to her; it sounded a long way down. 'Come on, slowcoach! It's not as bad when you get to the bottom – ha! If you'll pardon the expression!'

Hazel readied herself as Bramley dashed from one shoulder to the next, chewing frantically on his tail.

'Wait, Hazel . . . No, *please*! Think about what you're doing . . . I'll never be clean again, my nose will never recover, my fur will fall out, I just *know* it . . .'

Spreading her arms to better keep balance, she shuffled over the edge of the slope and began to slide down on her heels. Bramley grabbed her ear but Hazel didn't feel it. She gave a little scream as her boots skittered on the smooth and slimy stones. Down she went, somehow keeping her balance even as her descent got faster.

She wanted to slow down, but just couldn't bring herself to touch the slope with her bare hands. The smell . . . oh, the *smell*! Below she glimpsed green water and dark, glistening walls. Something, perhaps a loose stone or a crack, tripped her and Hazel pitched headfirst with her arms wheeling at her sides.

'Tit*uuuus*!'

Hard stone and brackish water rushed up to meet her. She threw up her hands, closed her eyes and prepared for impact. Strong arms caught and pulled her into an embrace; Hazel smelt warm fabric and tobacco smoke.

'All right, girl,' Titus said. 'I've got you.'

Breathless, Hazel emerged from the folds of Titus's coat. 'I'm blaming you for that, but thanks for catching me.'

They were on a narrow stone ledge next to a conduit filled with slow-flowing water. Shreds of evil-smelling mist drifted over the surface. The only light in the tunnel came from the room of easement high above. Bramley squeaked as a black rat emerged from a gap between the bricks, regarded them curiously, then slipped into the water.

'The castle sewer,' Titus said. 'A home from home for a slop-sprite like you. We're safe now. Just let your eyes adjust, and then we'll be on our way.'

'It's my nose I want to adjust,' Bramley said between little retches of disgust.

'Don't you dare be sick in my hair,' Hazel said, doing her best to breathe only through her mouth.

'Stop griping, you two. Hazel – you have the book? Let me see.'

Hazel took the *Necronomicon* from her trousers and handed it to him. Titus examined the cover and then opened it to the title page. 'This is it. Look here . . .'

'I can't read the words.'

'Indeed,' Titus said. 'Petrov was Swedish. But it says: *The Necronomicon. Being a Truthful Account of a Far Traveller into the Long Reaches of the Underworld. As recorded by Lars Göran Petrov.*'

Hazel stared in wonder at the bold gothic script and for a moment she forgot the darkness, even the appalling smell, and laughed. 'And we got it right from under their noses!'

'We're one step closer,' Titus said. 'Look – there's a faint light down there. Might be our way out. Follow me, and don't slip into the water because I won't be going in after you.'

Hazel followed, keeping as close to the wall as she could without actually touching it. The foetid odour faded, but she couldn't tell if it was because they were reaching cleaner air, or because she was getting used to it.

Titus stopped so unexpectedly that Hazel ran into the back of him. 'I am coming with you, you know. Into the Underworld.'

'Titus,' she said, regaining her balance. 'I know you want to protect me, and I . . . I appreciate it. But I'll not drag you into any more danger. That's a path for me to take alone.'

'Alone?' Bramley squeaked, 'But you'll take me, won't you?'

Hazel plucked him from her hair. 'I've been thinking about this whole thing, especially now that I'm so close, and I've come to a decision. I don't want *either* of you coming with me. It's too dangerous, and you've already risked so much on my behalf.' She took a deep breath. 'So, there you have it. I'm going on my own. Decision made.'

Bramley and Titus exchanged a look, then stared angrily back at her.

'Ridiculous,' Bramley snapped. 'Leave me behind? How dare you even *think* such a thing?'

'Out of the bloody question,' Titus added.

Hazel opened her mouth to protest but Titus interrupted. 'You either agree to let us come with you, or we won't tell you how you can obtain the demon blood needed to draw the magic circle.'

'But—'

'We're coming with you,' Bramley said. 'And it's two against one, so there.'

'He's right,' Titus said. 'We started this story together, and we'll finish it together, no matter how it ends.' And with that final statement he walked on towards a distant circle of light, leaving Hazel smiling with relief.

32
BACK TO THE LAIR ...

Witches slay cattle, blast the produce of the earth,
the fruit of the trees, the grape from the vine.
Crimes, Heresies and Misdemeanours by Sir Stefan de Crouché

It was a long walk back to the Bannered Mare, and by the time the companions dragged themselves up the back steps the sun was crowning the rooftops and the city was beginning to stir.

Hazel was exhausted and wanted to sleep for a week – but not before she had washed. She found the tavern bath in the laundry room, filled it with pump water which she warmed with gentle blasts of magic, and scrubbed away the filth and stink of the sewer.

Feeling a hundred times better but hardly able to keep her eyes open, she got dressed and stumbled back to her room. Bramley was fast asleep under a fold of the bedclothes. Titus sat at the table poring over the book.

'Let me see,' she muttered, shuffling towards him.

'You need to sleep,' Titus said. 'Bed. Now.'

'I want to read it . . .'

Titus snapped the book closed. 'Fluent in Swedish, are you? No? Thought not. *Bed.*'

With uncharacteristic obedience, Hazel scooped up her sleeping familiar and crawled under the covers.

A persistent scratching sound roused her from sleep. She stretched, yawned and opened her eyes. Golden sunlight fell on Titus, who was still sitting at the table writing notes with a quill. His hair was loose, his coat crumpled – his usual scruffiness had returned.

'What time is it?' she said.

Titus didn't look up. 'About two in the afternoon.'

'Huh. But what day? I feel like I've slept for a week.'

'Same day,' Bramley said from his perch on the inkpot. 'There's bacon and eggs over there.'

Famished, Hazel grabbed the plate and joined them by the window. The *Necronomicon* lay open on the table. Dense print covered its pages and the margins were filled with Titus's notes and translations.

'Does it tell us what we need to know?' Hazel's heart fluttered with trepidation. 'Does it tell us how to open the gate?'

'It does. It's all here – a diagram of the magic circle, instructions on where to place it, and –' he flipped back a few pages – 'see this? That's the spell that opens the gate.'

Hazel peered closer. Inside a border adorned with skulls and bones was a short block of text written in ugly, spiky letters.

'This spell is written in the language of the demons,' Titus said, turning his dark eyes on to her. 'And in order

177

for it to work the recitation must be exact – every word pronounced with absolute precision.'

'All right,' Hazel said, taken aback by the vehemence in his voice. 'So we'll be careful . . .'

'You don't understand. I have a loose grasp of their hideous tongue, but not enough to be able to speak it with the accuracy this spell demands.'

'Titus told me that if we say the spell incorrectly the results could be catastrophic,' Bramley said, hopping off the inkpot and clambering up to Hazel's shoulder. 'We might open a gate that lets demons *into* our world.'

Hazel slumped on to the bed. 'I don't want that.'

'Of course you don't,' Titus said. 'But you see the problem? None of us can read the spell without creating enormous risk to others.'

Bramley nuzzled Hazel's neck reassuringly. 'But we know a man who can.'

'You don't mean . . . ?' Hazel's eyes widened. '*Murrell?*'

Titus shrugged. 'Who else? He's the only man alive who speaks the language well enough to open a gate. We know this because we saw him do it at Rivenpike.'

'But he's locked up, and due to be executed this weekend,' Hazel said, throwing her hands up in despair.

'We know,' Bramley said, 'but while you've been snoring *we've* come up with a plan.'

'Indeed,' Titus said. 'Now, the *Necronomicon* says that the magic circle must be drawn "in a place steeped in misery and death". And look here.' He held up a poster adorned with a striking picture of a sneering Murrell.

'It's an advertisement for the Execution Pageant,' Hazel said.

'Yes, and they're being delivered by the Order all over the neighbourhood. I picked this up from the taproom downstairs. It says that Murrell is to be executed in the arena on Tower Hill.' Titus leaned forward. 'I've been there many times over the years, and there are tiers of seats facing a platform in the middle where the condemned meet their fate.'

'So?' Hazel said, wishing he'd get to the point.

'So, if *I* can copy the magic circle under the platform, and *you* can convince Murrell to recite the spell during his own execution, then he *might* be able to open the gate into the Underworld.'

Hazel stared at him and then slowly said, 'I don't know whether it's the most brilliant or the most foolhardy idea I've ever heard.'

'A bit of both I think,' Titus replied. 'Bramley and I have been racking our brains, and frankly, it's the only thing we think has any hope of working.'

'Murrell is the only man who can recite the spell – we need him to do it,' Bramley said. 'But rescuing him from the Island is impossible, so we wait for the Witch Hunters to bring him to us, at the Pageant, and over the magic circle.'

'But how can I convince Murrell to help us at his own execution?'

'Oh, he'll help us all right,' Titus smiled. 'That's the beauty of the whole idea: creating a demon gate at his own execution is Murrell's best – hell, his *only* – chance of escape.'

'Imagine it, Hazel,' Bramley said. 'Swirling magic, the ground opening up beneath the pyre . . . It'll be chaos, pandemonium. The Witch Hunters will flee in terror – imagine the look on Hopkins' face! – and we can use the distraction to go through the gate.'

The more Hazel thought about the idea the more sense it made. 'And Murrell?'

Titus waved his hand. 'Who cares? He can make his getaway and go where he wants.'

'There's still the matter of getting the demon blood, of course,' Bramley said.

'But we have a plan for that too,' Titus said, and he told Hazel about the trip to the Guild Master, the plague doctor murdered and buried in his own garden, and the demon using his uniform as a disguise. 'So I track down this demon, kill it, and harvest its blood.'

'Which we can use for the magic circle,' Hazel breathed.

'Exactly. Your job is to get Murrell to help. Does he know about his execution?'

'He didn't when I left him.'

'You'll have to tell him then.' Titus took out a clasp knife, cut the spell page from the book and handed it to Hazel. 'And give him this.'

Hazel took it and said, 'I'm going back, aren't I?'

180

Titus nodded. 'If you want your mother safe, then yes, I'm afraid so.'

Hazel felt the strength drain out of her; the idea of returning to the Order and immersing herself in the bleakness of their world was almost too much to bear.

'Listen, Hazel,' Titus said gently. 'There's no shame in changing your mind. Your mother would understand.'

Hazel pictured her mother's smile and imagined the joy at seeing it again. She straightened her spine. 'I'm going back.'

'And this time I'm coming with you,' Bramley said.

'Very well. Don't worry about that demon either,' Titus growled. 'It'll be no match for me.'

Hazel looked down at her hands. 'I don't know what to say,' she said, feeling a tremor in her voice. 'You've both done so much . . .'

'No tears, foolish girl!' Titus said. 'Your mother is depending on us, so now is the time for *action*. The first thing to do is get you back inside the Tower . . .'

33
...WHERE THE DRAGONS RESIDE

'The rebels comprise of witches, Wielders, and soldiers still loyal to dead King Charles. We underestimate them at our peril.'
General Charles Fleetwood

A few hours later, under a sweltering mid-afternoon sun, Hazel once again approached the outer walls of the Tower of London.

'Remember to act confused, but be you,' Bramley whispered from deep in her hair. 'You as in William, that is. The main thing is we want them to know that Murrell's magical hold over you has gone.'

Making sure she looked suitably dishevelled, Hazel approached the guards. They recognized her immediately. 'It's him!' one cried, grabbing his halberd. 'The General's apprentice, the one who was bewitched.'

People nearby looked alarmed and began to back away. The other guard was already pointing his matchlock at Hazel, and the look of terror on his face made her think he was going to shoot her dead in the street. 'Don't you move,' he commanded.

Hazel stopped and held her hands out in front of her. 'Please, I'm better now—'

'Quiet, or I'll shoot you where you stand.'

'He's terrified,' Bramley squeaked. 'And I don't like the way his hands are shaking . . .'

'All right, Ned,' the other guard said. 'Go and fetch the General. Quick, now.' He approached Hazel with his halberd lowered. 'As for you, boy, get in the guardhouse until it's decided what's to be done.'

Hazel nodded and slowly made her way to the little stone guardhouse built into the gate. As soon as she was inside, the guard locked the door behind her. She sat at the table, trying to catch her breath: that guard had been only a whisker away from killing her.

'That was close,' Bramley said. 'Now you need to convince the General you're back to being you.'

Hazel waited, watching dust motes dance in the sunlight. *News of my return will spread, watchful Thorn will get wind of it and he'll come and find me,* she thought. *Then I pass my message on to Murrell.*

She flinched as the door opened. Light streamed in, followed by Hopkins, Grimstone, and three wary guards who took up position behind her. Grimstone barred the door, one hand resting on the butt of his pistol. Hopkins sat opposite and held her gaze for an uncomfortably long time.

'I've come back, General,' Hazel said.

'I can see that,' Hopkins said quietly. 'But who are you really? Are you Apprentice Lowe? Or are you a puppet of Murrell's, returned to cause mischief in my house?'

'It's me, I promise,' Hazel said, adding a pleading note

to her voice. 'His power over me, it's gone . . . I am myself again.'

Hopkins took his curved blade from his pocket and tapped it on the table. 'William, I saw you jump with what seemed like suicidal intent into the river. How can I be sure a spell powerful enough to compel you to do such a thing has simply . . . faded away?'

'The words Murrell spoke, the lies he told to compel me to jump – I don't hear them any more.' Hazel looked down as if ashamed. 'I wanted so much to show you I could succeed but all I've done is let you down. I'm sorry, General.'

'I think you'd better tell me what happened, William,' Hopkins said. 'From the moment you went in to see him.'

Hazel thought back to the story that she, Titus and Bramley had concocted back at the Bannered Mare and began to speak, haltingly, with pauses and frowns, all the while careful to ensure it didn't sound rehearsed.

Hopkins and Grimstone listened as she told them about how Murrell had spoken to her in his cell; about the overwhelming urge to jump in the river; about the choking water and pulling tide, and how her desire to live had driven her to swim for shore; about wandering confused through the streets, yet slowly making her way back to the Tower to be among her people again.

'Well, Grimstone?' Hopkins said when she'd finished. 'What do you think?'

'He appears to be back to normal – lucid, clear-eyed, calm.'

'Agreed,' Hopkins said, putting the blade back in his pocket.

Hazel's burgeoning relief withered and died when Grimstone added, 'But I've yet to fulfil my check on his story, General. The Spymaster is still insisting we go through that whole rigmarole.'

Of course! Hazel thought, feeling Bramley stiffen in fear. *How could I have been so careless as to forget that?*

'What's taking so long, Grimstone?' Hopkins snapped.

'I'm afraid the record office in Putney has suffered a fire and most of the registers have been destroyed. My administrators are sifting through the remains, but it will take time. In the interim we can move William to a cell until we've verified his story.'

Grimstone nodded to the guards, who moved in to grab Hazel's arms. A thrill of panic ran through her – she couldn't afford to get locked up. *But if I fight my way out now I'll lose my chance of being at Murrell's execution and entering the demon gate . . .*

'Belay that – I've had enough of the Spymaster's interference.' Hopkins waved the guards off. 'William, Murrell tried to make you drown yourself, just to spite me. I see your survival and loyal return to me as a victory of the good over the malign.' He smiled. 'It proves my faith in you was well founded.'

'So . . . you'll have me back? As your apprentice?' Hazel asked, feeling her hope return.

'Oh, you're more than just an apprentice.' Hopkins

185

laughed, leading her out into the sunshine. 'You're the prodigal son returned to the family fold!'

Hopkins accompanied Hazel back to her room. 'Light work for you today while you get your strength back,' he said. 'I'll send Anthony up with some paper-work – in the meantime you'd better put on a clean uniform.'

The room was just as she'd left it, although it felt like a lifetime had passed since she had last been there. *And I certainly never expected to return,* she thought forlornly as she closed the door, plucked Bramley from her hair and put him on the windowsill.

'Keep an eye out for Thorn,' she said.

Bramley pressed his nose against the glass. 'Let's just hope he knows where to find us.'

Hazel tried to order her thoughts as she changed. She and Titus had so much to do and to get exactly right for the plan to work, and she hated that so much was being left to chance. But it was pointless to worry about things outside her control.

I have to do my best, and make damn sure my best is good enough.

Bramley hid behind the curtain as someone knocked on the door. Hazel opened it and found Anthony outside with a stack of papers in his arms.

'Hello, William,' he said. 'I can't tell you how pleased I am to see you again.'

Hazel smiled, her spirits lifting. 'Me too. Are you settling in yet?'

'I'm trying to.' Anthony put the papers on the desk; he seemed relieved to be rid of them. 'These are death certificates,' he said in a hushed voice. 'For all the witch prisoners who are to be burned at the Pageant this weekend.'

Hazel stared at the pile in horror. 'But there are so many . . .'

Anthony looked up and down the corridor and then closed the door. 'I counted them. There are three hundred and sixty-four certificates there – all the witches in the hulk and the Tower.'

Hazel struggled to even picture that number of people. It was enough to fill a hall, a street – there were whole *villages* with fewer people. And Hopkins was going to murder them all: mothers, daughters, sisters . . .

Just for being different. Just for being witches, or those who sympathized with them.

She was gripped by an anger so intense it made her heart thrum with magic.

'Three hundred and sixty-four?' she said. 'But how are they going to kill so many at once?'

'They're going to lock them all below decks in the hulk and then shoot fire arrows to set it alight.' Anthony swallowed. 'People can watch from the riverbanks as they . . . burn.'

'I just can't believe it.'

'I know. I can't sleep for thinking about it,' Anthony said, close to tears. 'The General says it's the right thing to do but . . . I just don't understand how that can be.'

'Here, come and sit down.' Hazel felt him shaking as she helped him into a chair.

'And there's something else,' he whispered. 'I've found out why Grimstone chose me to join the Order.'

'Oh?'

'It's about that prisoner they're always going on about, Nicolas Murrell. You know he's to be burned at the stake as well?'

'Yes, I know,' Hazel said gently. 'Go on.'

'Well, the General, he wants *me* to light the pyre.'

'You?' It took a moment for the words to sink in. 'But why?'

'He says the sight of an innocent boy ridding the world of an evil man like Murrell is a powerful lesson for the nation,' Anthony said, wiping his streaming eyes. 'But I don't know what that *means*. All I know is that I don't want to kill anybody, no matter how evil they are.'

He broke down, sobbing piteously, narrow shoulders heaving. Not knowing what else to do, Hazel put her arms around him and waited for him to stop.

34
A BIRD IN THE HAND

'The Black Widow – they say she glows all the time
like fiery embers, although I have never seen her.'
Witch Hunter Sergeant Josiah Hart

When Anthony had calmed down, Hazel walked him back to his room with comforting words that she knew wouldn't help. She found it hard to believe how anyone could ask a boy like Anthony to set light to an execution pyre; the fact that if her plan to open the demon gate was successful, Anthony wouldn't have to set light to anything didn't stop her blood from boiling.

Back in her room, she leaned her elbows on the windowsill and stared past the Tower's suffocating layers of defence. The sun was low, blooding the distant rooftops red. She was tired, and angry, and frightened.

Bramley crawled down her arm and perched on her clasped hands. 'You can't save Anthony too, you know. So try not to think about it.'

'I can't help it. And all those witches . . . they're going to *die.*'

'I know,' Bramley said, shaking his head sadly. 'It's monstrous.'

189

Hazel took a deep breath. 'Bram, I've made a decision.'

'Oh dear . . .'

'I'm going to find a way to help them.' She nodded with conviction. 'Yes. That's what I'm going to do.'

'Oh, Hazel,' Bramley cried, fur bristling with frustration.

'I can't simply stand aside and let it happen. All those lives!' A halo of angry magic flickered around her head. 'I won't let it happen.'

'But have you thought about *how*?'

Something fluttered on to the windowsill outside and tapped on the glass.

'Look,' Hazel said. 'It's Thorn!'

'Thank goodness,' Bramley said as she threw open the window. 'We deserve a bit of luck.'

The little robin hopped inside and perched on Hazel's finger. 'Greetings, Hazel Hooper. Greetings, Hazel's mouse.'

'My name's *Bramley*.'

'The whole Tower is talking about your reappearance,' Thorn said. 'So naturally Nicolas is interested to know what precipitated it.'

Hazel looked blank.

'He means what *caused* you to return?' Bramley muttered.

'Oh, right . . . Well, it's like this, see . . .'

And so, with Bramley sitting in one hand and Thorn balanced on the other, Hazel explained the plan to enable Murrell to recite the demon spell and open the gate at his own execution.

190

Thorn listened attentively, head cocked and shrewd eyes shining. When Hazel had finished he said, 'And in return for Nicolas's service . . .'

'He gets a fair chance at escaping death,' Bramley snapped. 'He should be *grateful*.'

'I understand that,' Thorn said mildly. 'And I feel sure this is an opportunity he will embrace wholeheartedly.'

Hazel narrowed her eyes. 'Murrell must have known that we'd not be able to recite the spell properly. So why didn't he tell me that before?'

'He told you what you asked to know, no more, no less.'

'He knew we'd come back, didn't he?' Hazel said hotly.

Thorn stretched out a wing before replying. 'He suspected as much, but he did not know. Besides, he is not the only one who withheld information. *Is* he, Hazel Hooper?'

'I don't know what you mean . . .'

'You didn't mention his final appearance at the Execution Pageant, did you?'

Hazel flushed. 'I . . . No, I didn't.'

'See?' Thorn said, hopping on to the windowsill. 'We all keep secrets from time to time, when it suits us.'

Hazel and Bramley shared a look; Thorn was even more perceptive than they'd previously thought.

'But what of the magic circle?' Thorn asked. 'Will it be ready in time?'

'I hope so.' Hazel took out the folded page of the *Necronomicon*. 'This is the spell. Can you carry it to Murrell?'

'No need. He knows it by heart.'

'He knows it by . . . ?' Angry sparks crackled through Hazel's hair. 'Dammit, he knows everything about the gate, doesn't he? The spell, the placement of the magic circle?'

'That's true, Hazel Hooper,' Thorn said. 'But there's no cause to become angry – in the end you both want the same thing, just for different reasons.'

'We want to get into the Underworld, Murrell wants to escape,' Bramley said.

'Serendipitous, don't you think?' Thorn fluttered to the window. 'Now I must tell Nicolas the details of your plan . . .'

'Wait!' Hazel said. 'I have a friend: Titus White.'

Thorn turned back to her. 'Nicolas has spoken to me about him.'

'Can you take a message to him right away? I'd like him to know that I'm back in the Tower, and that Nicolas has agreed to help us.'

'Very well,' the little bird said. 'Tell me where to find him . . .'

35
A FINGER BECKONS

The sun swung its beams around the room as Titus pored over the *Necronomicon*. Hours bled into each other, but he hardly noticed, so intent was he on memorizing the eye-watering patterns and symbols that made up the magic circle he was going to have to copy.

When the light in the room turned grey he leaned back and dug the heels of his hands into his eyes. He was waiting for night to fall so he could go out and hunt the demon, knowing that his chances of finding it were slim.

There was a knock at the door, so he covered the *Necronomicon* with a cloth and got up to open it. Mrs Treacher was standing outside.

'This was just delivered for you,' she said, passing him a package and a sealed letter.

'Thank you,' Titus said, and closed the door.

He put the package on the desk, opened the letter and began to read:

Dear Mr White,

I fear that writing this letter may be the last meaningful thing I do before this blasted plague takes me - I fervently hope it will make a difference.

Another dead girl has been found, this time in the abandoned meat-packing district in Southwark docks. In the knowledge that I had examined the other victims, the Gatherers of the Dead brought her sad remains to me.

She bore the same expression of fear as the others, but this one was a fighter - upon close examination I found something clutched in her hand, something that proves beyond doubt that the killer is not of our world.

I've put it in the package. Open it when you are alone. I implore you to use your courage and skills to rid the city of this killer.

See you on the other side,
Sebastian

With growing excitement, Titus cut the string from the package and allowed the paper wrapping to unfold. Inside was a plain wooden box. Using the tip of his knife, he flipped the lid open.

'Good God,' he breathed.

A severed finger, six inches long from nail to knuckle, lay on a bed of straw. The skin was pinkish white, stretched tight over the bones, and marbled with thin, blue veins.

Titus lifted the grisly appendage from the box, wrinkling his nose at the stink of sour milk. The joints creaked when he bent them. The skin was cold and slick like wet glass. After a few minutes of close examination and cross-referencing what he discovered with *Demonologie*, he put it back in the box, closed the lid and took a shuddering breath.

He thought of the fight the victim must have put up, the desperate strength shown to actually rip off the finger, and felt saddened to his core. But at least now he knew exactly which demon he had to kill. He had its *name*.

Titus shuffled to the washstand to clean off the stink. He looked through the water at his hands. They still retained much of their old strength, but there was a tremor in them. Was it fear that caused it, or the weakness that came with age?

Whichever it is, I don't think I can defeat this enemy alone. Not any more.

His throat was dry. He wanted, *needed*, a drink. Danger, pain, death – he'd faced them a thousand times without blinking. What scared him was failure. He shrugged on his coat, checked his pistol and jammed his hat over his head.

'Get a hold of yourself,' he growled. 'And do your job.'

Something fluttered through the open window and landed on the bedstead. It was a robin with one lame leg and bright, intelligent eyes.

Titus raised his eyebrows. 'Well well,' he said. 'You must be Thorn.'

'That is right,' the little bird chirruped. 'And you are Titus White, the Witch Finder and friend of Hazel Hooper?'

'I am, and I warn you, bird, I'm not as trusting as she is. What do you want?'

'I have a message for you, from Nicolas Murrell.'

Titus's lip turned into a sneer. 'Go on.'

'He agrees with the plan to open the gate at the Pageant, and thanks you for the opportunity to right some of the wrongs he has caused in the past.'

Titus gripped the back of the chair with both hands. They felt steadier now. 'I'm doing this for Hazel, not for him.'

'I understand,' Thorn said, bobbing his head in acknowledgement. 'Nevertheless, he thanks you. And he wants to know how you are going to obtain the demon blood needed to draw the magic circle.'

'I'm working on it. In fact, little bird, you can come with me while I track it down.'

'Very well.'

'And then you can pass a message on to Hazel at the Tower, because I have a feeling I'm going to need her help to kill it . . .'

36
THE KILLING FLOOR

It was a hot night so Hazel had left the window open while sorting the death certificates into alphabetical order. She had read each name, imagining who they were and the terror they must be feeling at being trapped in the prison hulk awaiting death.

On the stroke of midnight, tired and sick to her stomach, she picked up the last certificate in the pile. She didn't think it was possible to feel any sadder until she read the name written in bold black letters at the top: 'David Drake, charged with colluding with witches and known criminals. Sentence: death.'

Beneath was a handwritten note:

> General, we have squeezed all the
> information we can from this boy – he is
> of no more use. I suggest we rid ourselves
> of his demon-tainted presence as soon as
> possible. I have already taken the liberty

of transferring him to the hulk in time for the Pageant.

Yours,
Interrogator Bloch

Hazel put the certificate down and rubbed her eyes. 'Oh, David,' she sighed. 'If only you'd stayed with us.'

She had already decided to find a way to rescue the prisoners, and knowing that David was now among them made her all the more determined. But *how* was she to do it?

A flutter of wings signalled the return of Thorn. 'I'm glad to find you awake, Hazel Hooper,' he said. 'I have a message from Titus White: he's found the demon's lair, and he requests your help in killing it . . .'

Fifteen minutes later, with Bramley clinging to her ear, Hazel followed Thorn from the Tower, across the bridge, and into the night-shrouded streets of Southwark. She was glad to be taking action; if what Titus said was right they might be able to get hold of the blood they needed this very night. There was just the small matter of killing a demon first.

Thorn hopped on to Hazel's shoulder when they reached a deserted crossroads just off Southwark High Road. 'Titus awaits you at the end of that alley. Now I must return to Nicolas and give him news of our endeavours. Good luck, Hazel Hooper.'

'Thank you, Thorn,' Hazel said. 'I've a feeling we're going to need it.'

The alley sloped down between shuttered and padlocked buildings. The entire district appeared abandoned, and Hazel realized why when she saw the red crosses on the doors.

'Plague's been busy in this neighbourhood,' Bramley said. 'I'll be glad to get out of this city, I can tell you.'

At the end of the alley was a dirty courtyard, fronted by dilapidated warehouses and an embankment dropping down to the river. Dry dung cut through with wagon tracks lay on the cobbles.

'Titus,' Hazel hissed. 'Where are you?'

'Right behind you.' The old Witch Finder emerged from a nearby doorway. 'Not very observant, are you?'

'Don't *do* that,' Bramley squeaked. 'My nerves are already shattered.'

Hazel reached up and pushed the hair away from Titus's face – he looked pale, haggard, ten years older than when she'd last seen him. 'What on earth has happened to you? You look terrible.'

'I'm fine,' he said, waving her away. 'Now listen to me carefully. Everything depends on what happens here, now, tonight. You must be ready.'

'Thorn told us you've tracked down the demon,' Hazel whispered, allowing Titus to draw her deeper into the shadows. 'Is that true?'

Titus knelt next to her and rested his hand on her

shoulder. The night cut deep lines into his face. 'See that warehouse over there? That's the creature's lair.'

'How do you know?'

'I discovered the identity of the demon we seek, which enabled me to use this.' Titus took the Entropy Monocle from his pocket. 'The tracks I found were faint, hard to follow, but as I suspected they led right up to our unfortunate plague doctor's house.'

'Why were the tracks so faint?' Bramley asked.

'Why do you think, furry-brain?' Titus said. 'They were old.'

'Ah,' Hazel said, 'because since putting on the doctor's robes and boots the demon's not left any tracks.'

'Exactly. The old trail to the doctor's door led back here.' Titus pointed to a broken window on the ground floor of a warehouse. 'Through that window, in fact. Fear not – our quarry isn't at home at present, but it'll be back before daybreak.'

Hazel suppressed a shiver of fear. 'You'd better tell me what we're dealing with.'

'The name of the demon we hunt is Bloodybones,' Titus said. 'A *daemon-mediocritas*, cunning and cruel. You've seen its size and form already. I just hope we don't have to face it unmasked – its features are by all accounts disconcerting.'

'Bloodybones . . . Yes, that's a fitting name,' Hazel said, remembering her encounter at the tavern. 'How did you find out its name?'

Titus told them about the finger found in the dead girl's

hand and how he'd used it, and the description Hazel had provided, to identify their dangerous quarry.

'And so tonight is our chance to rid London of this horror and get the blood we need for the magic circle,' Titus concluded. He picked up a bucket and a lantern from the doorway. 'Hazel, can you light this for me? Thanks ... Now, come with me. I want to show you what we need to do.'

Being careful not to cut herself on the glass, Hazel followed Titus through the broken window and into the warehouse.

The air was warm and left an unpleasant salty taste in her mouth.

The far walls were lost in darkness, and Hazel had the unnerving impression she was in a place without boundaries. Lantern light bounced from a forest of timber pillars and branching rafters as Titus headed deeper inside. 'This used to be a meat-packing warehouse,' he said, making his way past notched butcher's blocks and meat hooks dangling on chains. 'But it's been abandoned ever since this last outbreak of plague.'

'Perfect place to hide,' Bramley said from Hazel's shoulder, his whiskers twitching nervously. 'But who summoned this beast? And why?'

'Good questions, Master Mouse. But one thing at a time, eh?' He stopped in a cleared space where moonlight poured like milk through skylights far above. 'You are now standing in a magic circle – a trap I've made to catch our demon.'

Hazel looked down and saw faint lines and patterns on

the floor, forming a circle about ten paces across. 'Wait a moment – is this drawn in blood?'

'It is. The spell demands it.'

'And where did you get the blood?' Hazel stared at him in dawning horror. 'Oh, Titus! This is *yours*, isn't it?' She pulled up his coat sleeve to reveal a bandage around his arm.

Titus shrugged. 'Where else was I going to get human blood from at such short notice?'

'I don't know, but you shouldn't have used your own. No *wonder* you look about ready to keel over.'

'Now see here, my girl,' Titus growled, 'I'm as strong as ever I was and losing a few drops of blood . . .'

Hazel fumed. 'A few *drops*?'

'Hey, you two!' Bramley squeaked. 'Stop wasting time. In case you've forgotten, our friendly killer demon might come back at any moment.'

'Quite right, Master Mouse,' Titus said, pulling his sleeve back down. 'Now listen: as soon as Bloodybones crosses the edge of this circle a magic wall stronger than stone will rise up in less time than it takes to blink. In other words, make sure you get outside the circle before the demon enters.'

'Wait.' Bramley held up a paw. 'Why would we be inside the circle when the demon is so close?'

'I think, Bram,' Hazel said quietly, 'it's because for this plan to work I'm to be the bait that draws the demon into the trap.'

'*What?*' Bramley spluttered.

'I'm afraid so,' Titus said. 'This demon hunts children, and has already shown a special interest in Hazel. It won't be able to resist her.'

'All right,' Bramley fumed. 'Assuming we survive the predatory attentions of a vengeful demon and manage to trap it without being killed ourselves, what happens next?'

Titus removed the *Necronomicon* from his pocket. 'I read out a spell that will incapacitate the demon long enough for me to draw off its blood. After that I shoot a bullet into its heart and send its soul back to the Underworld. Understand?'

Hazel nodded. Bramley sulked.

'Good luck, slop-sprite.' Titus brushed the hair from her cheek. 'I won't be far away.'

37
BLOOD AND BONES

*'I am at heart a country gentleman, but there is no place for
gentility in this war against the witches.'*
Lord Protector Oliver Cromwell

'**A**nother fine mess,' Bramley muttered from his lookout
perch on top of Hazel's head.

'I know, Bram,' Hazel said. 'Why don't you go and find
Titus? No need for both of us to take this risk.'

'Don't be silly,' Bramley said, tapping his tail against her
forehead. 'I'm not leaving you to face this beast alone. Just
remember, the plan is to run away. Got it? *Run away.*'

'I understand.' She paced the circle, feeling trapped
and wary. 'Talk to me, Bram. Take my mind off this awful
waiting.'

'All right, here's a question for you. When are you going
to tell Titus that David is marked to die alongside all those
witches?'

'I don't know,' Hazel sighed. 'I'm dreading it. Titus will
just blame himself, even though David's fate is my fault, not
his.'

'Oh for goodness sake! I've never met such a couple of
martyrs as you and Titus. What does it matter whose fault it

is? You have to tell him – he has a right to know.'

'I know, I know. And I will, after we've got this over with. In fact, when he finds out about David he might be more willing to help me find a way to rescue the witches.'

'Oh yes, I'd all but forgotten about that fresh dose of insanity . . .' Bramley froze, then crawled slowly down to Hazel's shoulder. 'Look over there, by the main door. I think our demon is here.'

The light from the lantern at Hazel's feet did not reach far beyond the magic circle, but on the very edge of the surrounding darkness the plague doctor stood, perfectly still and watching her.

Her heart thudded in her throat, but she didn't take a single step backwards – everything depended on her doing what Titus had said. Meat hooks jangled, seconds dragged by, and the demon remained motionless except for a barely perceptible sway.

Hazel balanced on the balls of her feet and, unable to bear the wait any longer, cried, 'Well? Here I am. Come and get me!' But still the demon didn't move. Perhaps it knew about the trap.

'Something's wrong,' Bramley whispered. 'Look closely, Hazel – is it my imagination or is it floating?'

Hazel raised the lantern over her head, casting the light further into the darkness. There was a gap under the demon's robes where its boots should be – Bramley was right, it *was* floating.

'That's not Bloodybones,' Hazel breathed. 'Its just the

robe hanging from some chains.'

'So where . . . ?'

Movement overhead! And Hazel looked up into a pair of bloodshot and protuberant eyes. Bloodybones, human in form yet gruesomely thin, hung upside down from a rafter, close enough for Hazel to feel its cold breath against her face.

'Red Witch,' it hissed, tongue squirming behind blunt grey teeth. 'Found you!'

Pure shock caused Hazel to duck – a second before Bloodybones lashed out. Claws sliced the air barely an inch from her nose. The white demon grinned, writhing towards her like a maggot on a hook.

'Hazel, get out of there!' Titus shouted from the darkness.

Bloodybones unclasped one of its feet from the rafter and began to lower its leg to the floor. Hazel wanted to move, but the demon seemed to hold her to the spot with its terrible eyes. White hot pain shot through her ear, strong enough to make her scream and break the spell.

With Bramley still clinging by his teeth to her ear, Hazel threw herself under the demon and rolled over the edge of the circle just as its foot touched the ground. The air hummed as a shimmering wall of magic reached up to the ceiling far above, trapping Bloodybones inside.

Hazel slowly clambered to her feet. 'You can let go now, Bram,' she said, lifting him away from her punctured ear. 'We've done it.'

Titus puffed up to her. 'Are you all right? That was far too close.'

'I'm fine,' Hazel replied with a rueful smile. She took the handkerchief offered by Titus and dabbed it against her throbbing ear. 'Thanks to Bram.'

They approached the magic circle and peered through its crackling layers.

Bloodybones pressed its hands on the other side of the wall. 'Red Witch, I see you.'

'But you can't *get* me,' Hazel said, feeling a hot flash of anger. 'And now we've stopped your murdering ways forever.'

'I've had my fill of childish souls,' it replied, licking its lips. 'I'll return home . . . sated.'

'You won't return anywhere,' Bramley said. 'We're going to kill you for what you've done.'

'You will not,' Bloodybones said, 'for I am of demon-kind. You may destroy this flesh, this bone, but my soul will live on.'

'Who summoned you, Bloodybones?' Titus said.

'I know not her name, but she wielded magic that froze the air.'

Hazel swallowed. 'Why were you summoned?'

'For one purpose – to find *you*, the Red Witch, the one who burns.' The demon snapped its teeth together. 'And gorge upon your soul!'

'So why hunt the others if you were here for her?' Titus said, bristling with anger.

'Why not?' Bloodybones' laugh gurgled from deep in its throat. 'The summoner's spells were too weak to hold my appetite in check. So I . . . *feasted*.'

Hazel clenched her fists, trying to control her anger. 'Your summoner, where is she now?'

'She is my prisoner, held captive in the slaughter room yonder.'

Titus drew Hazel aside. 'The wall won't last much longer – it's time for me to get rid of this monster. Wait for me outside while I do my work.'

Hazel couldn't take her eyes off the grinning demon. 'I want to watch.'

'I know,' Titus said. 'But I don't want you to see me do this. Go. For me.' He gave her a gentle shove towards the door. 'I'll come for you when I'm done and we'll face the summoner together.'

Hazel reluctantly did as he asked, and was just climbing through the window when the demon started to scream.

38
A BOLD PROPOSITION

*'The demon he beckoned, the demon he spoke,
the demon he led me until I awoke.'*
The heretic Alex Hellid before his execution

'**I**t's her, isn't it?' Hazel said, angrily kicking stones towards the river. '*She* summoned Bloodybones to kill me. For revenge.'

'It makes sense,' Bramley said from her shoulder. 'After all, you did kill her demon – and in a very messy fashion, I might add.'

'All those children dead.' Hazel felt numb. 'Because of me.'

Bramley gave her already punctured ear a nip.

'Ow! Stop *doing* that!'

'Well, if you will say such ridiculous things,' Bramley snapped. 'What happened is her fault, and hers alone. She summoned and set Bloodybones loose, not you. She's the person responsible for those deaths.'

She. Her. Hazel could not bring herself to say the name out loud.

Lilith Kilbride.

Lilith Kilbride who had been Murrell's Frost Witch

consort and most trusted companion. Hazel had hardly given her a thought since leaving her tied up and unconscious in Murrell's lair during their escape from the Coven all those weeks ago.

'I still feel responsible,' Hazel muttered, sitting down and dangling her legs over the jetty.

'What should we do with her, assuming she's still alive?' Bramley said, jumping on to her lap.

'Titus will probably want to execute her himself.'

'More death?' Bramley twitched his whiskers in consternation. 'Killing her makes us no better than that demon she summoned. No, we can't allow that.'

'No, of course not.' Hazel sighed. 'But she has to pay for what she's done.'

'You mean punish her? But how?'

'I don't know . . . But something to atone for the damage she's caused.'

'I don't think that's possible, Hazel. Damage can be repaired, death can't. Besides, she might not even want to atone.'

The faint cries of the demon stopped, leaving just the gentle lap of the water around the jetty posts and the cry of gulls overhead.

'Maybe we could get her to help us,' Hazel said at last.

'*Help* us?' Bramley spluttered. 'She's been trying to kill you!'

'I know, but we do have common causes, don't we?' She pointed to the prison hulk and then the Island. 'Rescuing

210

the witches *and* Murrell, the man she loves.'

'But how could we trust her not to have another go at you? Perhaps we should just leave her where she is . . .'

Hazel shook her head. 'Bloodybones said Lilith summoned him to kill me, and me alone. He only hunted those other girls because her spells were too weak to contain his urges.'

'So?'

'So she probably feels terrible about the damage she's caused. Terrible enough perhaps to have reconsidered her thirst for revenge.'

'You don't know that, Hazel,' Bramley said, shaking his head. 'That woman must be mad to have done what she did. Working alongside her, even if she agrees to help, well, it's too much of a risk.'

'We'll only know for sure when we talk to her,' Hazel said, smoothing down Bramley's bristling fur. 'I just think that a powerful Wielder like Lilith would be useful to us. And heaven knows we need all the help we can get.'

'He'll never agree, you know . . .' Bramley said. 'Oh, speak of the devil!'

There was a clank as Titus set the bucket down on the ground behind them. 'It's done. There's more than enough blood there to draw the circle.'

'Come and sit down,' Hazel said, looking up at his grey face. 'You look exhausted.'

Titus slowly lowered himself next to Hazel. They sat in silence for a while, watching the stars fade and the morning sun bathe the river in pale light, both thinking it was far too beautiful a day to herald the impending horror of the Execution Pageant.

Bramley peered at Titus from the crook of Hazel's arm. 'The demon – it's gone?'

'Aye,' Titus nodded. 'The spell worked, the demon's dead, its soul flung back to the Underworld, and we have its blood.'

'Thank you,' Hazel said.

'I did what had to be done. After that ordeal, drawing the magic circle in the arena will be easy.' He tapped Hazel on the knee. 'Now listen, you need to make sure you're close enough tonight to run into the gate as soon as it opens. I'll be under the platform waiting for you – with some provisions, of course.'

'Titus, I . . .' Hazel began.

'I can hardly believe I'm following in the footsteps of men like Petrov,' Titus said, shaking his shaggy head. 'Or Murrell.'

'Titus, *listen*! I need to talk to you. It's important.'

The old Witch Finder raised his eyebrows. 'Something tells me I'm not going to like this.'

'No,' Hazel sighed. 'You're not.' She pointed at the prison hulk moored in the shadow of Cromwell Island. 'There are three hundred and sixty-four witches on board that ship, and they are all to be executed tonight.'

'*All* of them?' Titus gasped.

'On Cromwell's orders,' Bramley said. 'We saw the

death certificates ourselves.'

'They're going to set it alight with the prisoners locked below,' Hazel said. 'The Order wants everyone in London to see the flames.'

Titus balled his hands into fists. 'Can we stop this? When's it happening?'

'Tonight, about an hour before Murrell's execution.'

'Tonight? Then there's no time for us to . . .' He turned to look at Hazel. 'Now wait a minute, girl – we agreed that I was to come with you into the Underworld.'

'I know we did.'

'Good,' Titus growled. 'So that means there's no chance of you suggesting that I rescue those witches and leave you to go into that terrible place alone?'

'I'm not suggesting anything.' Hazel looked down at her hands. 'How can I? I know it's an impossible choice for you to make.'

'There's no choice, Hazel. I'm coming with you, just like we agreed. I'm sorry for those witches, of course I am, but I cannot go back on my word.'

'Hazel?' Bramley said. 'You need to . . .'

'I know, Bram, but it's difficult.' She laid her hand on Titus's. 'There's something else you need to know. About David.'

Titus tensed, as if preparing to be struck. 'What about him?'

'He's a prisoner on the hulk too. He'll die with the rest if we don't do something about it.'

'Why . . .' His voice cracked across the word. '*Why* did you tell me that?'

'I had to. This is David we're talking about.'

Titus got up and stalked to the end of the jetty, head down, shoulders slumped. 'You're certain? He's on that hulk right now?'

'He is,' Hazel replied. 'David told the Order everything he knew about you, me, Murrell, the Coven. And after they'd squeezed him dry they threw him aside.'

Titus stared out at the glittering water. A few boats plied the waves: early-morning wherries, a portly cargo ship tacking upstream towards the docks, a flat-bottomed lighter piled high with hay bales.

Hazel waited, running her finger down Bramley's back, hating herself for adding more misery on to the man who had already done so much for her.

'There's no right or wrong answer,' Titus said. 'What do you think I should do?'

Hazel got up and joined him. 'I told you before we got to London that I'd be all right on my own. I have Bramley, and my wits.'

'I can't let him die in there – he's just a *boy* and I'm responsible for him.' He shook his head. 'But dammit, girl, I'm responsible for you, too.'

'No you're not. I employed your services as a Witch Finder to help me find Ma, remember?'

'So?' Titus growled.

'So, now I release you from our agreement.' She waved

214

her hand. 'You are free to go and do as you will.'

Titus scowled at her. 'That doesn't help.'

'I know.' Hazel smiled. 'I'm just trying to stop you from bashing yourself over the head and make a decision.'

Titus stood up straight, like an old tree shaking loose years of creeping brambles. 'I will help David, and all those other poor souls.'

Hazel leaned into him. 'Good.'

'But how?' Titus said, looking at the prison hulk. 'How can I possibly rescue all those people before tonight?'

'Ah, well, I've been thinking about that,' Hazel said, walking him back towards the warehouse. 'And I have an idea.'

'But as usual, Titus,' Bramley added, 'you're not going to like it.'

39
THE SLAUGHTER ROOM

*'There must be good grounds for the prevailing
belief that witches are evil; otherwise Parliament
would not have legislated against them.'*
Lord Edward Coke

Hazel was about to open the slaughter-room door when Titus put his hand on her arm. 'This is a mistake,' he said. 'We should kill her for what she did.'

The angry part of Hazel agreed: revenge would feel good. But the thoughtful part knew it would not make right the past, heal old wounds, or bring back the dead.

'No, we're here to talk to her,' she said. 'Everyone deserves a chance to explain.' Titus opened his mouth to protest but Hazel held up her hand. 'You didn't just go around shooting people when you were a Witch Finder, did you? You gave them a fair trial, right?'

'That's true, but we already know what she did,' Titus said.

'Are you forgetting what we talked about outside? We might be able to get her to help us.'

'Why would she help? She hates us. For pity's sake, she tried to have you *killed*.'

'I know that, but when she learns we're working with

her beloved Murrell she might come round.'

'Well, whatever you choose to do, for heaven's sake be careful,' Bramley squeaked from deep in Hazel's hair. 'This is a Frost Witch we're dealing with.'

'She has to pay for what she did,' Titus said.

'I know, but perhaps she can achieve that by doing some good.' Hazel put her hand on his arm. 'Please, let's just talk to her.'

'All right,' Titus growled, undoing the bolt. 'But should she give me any cause to put a bullet between her eyes you won't be able to stop me.'

A gust of warm air and animal manure wafted out as he opened the iron-panelled door. They slowly ventured into a low-ceilinged and windowless room. Red-stained gutters ran across the floors to drainage holes in each corner.

In the centre of the room was another magic circle, this one drawn in crude, bold strokes with some sort of black fluid. Tied to a pole in the middle shivered a black-haired woman in a filthy dress. They could not see her face because she was resting her forehead against drawn-up knees, but they recognized her straight away.

'No more, please,' Lilith whimpered. 'Can't you leave this world in peace?'

'Bloodybones is dead,' Hazel said. 'It's us you face now.'

Lilith looked up, her eyes wide with shock. 'Titus? *Hazel?* But how . . . ?'

'We tracked your demon here,' Titus said, shaking with rage. 'But only after it killed four innocent children.'

The Frost Witch managed to shuffle up the pole and stand on her own two feet. 'You've come to kill me,' she said, raising her chin. 'Go ahead. I can't fight you even if I wanted to – this magic circle negates my magic.'

'I'd love to kill you,' Titus said, curling his lip. 'But my friend here wants to talk to you first. Hazel?'

An image of Bloodybones seared into Hazel's mind and she thought of the girls who had died at his hand. The control she had over her anger shattered in an instant. Her skin glowed and fire burst around her. Titus staggered away, shielding his face from the baking heat.

Lilith did not flinch. 'Do it, girl,' she said. 'I deserve nothing less for what I did.'

'Hazel,' Bramley said, stroking her neck with his tail. 'Remember what you said about revenge.'

Hazel breathed deeply, sloughing off her hatred like a dead skin and feeling relief from the moment she did so. Her fire faded and retreated back inside, although she felt it burning still in the darkest part of her soul.

'You know what you did,' she said quietly to Lilith. 'You know who paid the price for your actions.'

Lilith nodded. Her voice shook when she spoke. 'I do. Bloodybones taunted me with their deaths. I couldn't stop him, or escape, much as I desired to.'

'You summoned him to kill me?'

'Yes. And there is nothing in my whole life that I regret more.'

'I think you'd better tell us what happened,' Titus said.

'And remember, your life hangs by a thread, so no lies.'

'Death is no threat to one in such torment as I,' Lilith replied. 'But I will tell you how I ended up here.'

'We left you tied up in Rivenpike,' Titus said. 'What happened when you woke up?'

'I followed your trail into the forest, but by the time I caught up, the Witch Hunters had arrested Nicolas and you were following them to London – although I couldn't guess why you would do so.' She looked at them enquiringly.

'We'll tell you later, but only after you finish your sorry tale,' Titus said. 'Continue.'

'I was eaten alive with hatred. You had already killed my demon, Spindle, my most loyal familiar, and now my beloved Nicolas was in the hands of the Order.' Lilith squeezed her eyes shut. 'The thought of the torments those monsters would heap on him drove me mad. I knew I couldn't rescue him, but I could *avenge* him.'

Hazel crouched down in front of the wretched Wielder, with Bramley perched on her shoulder. 'And so?'

'I needed time to prepare so I rushed ahead, cutting through forests, sleeping in ditches, until I arrived in this foul city about a month ago. I found this abandoned place and used all my skills to summon a demon fit to hunt you down.'

'Bloodybones,' Titus said.

'Bloodybones.' Lilith swiped away a tear. 'I tried to bind him to my will, to impose control and ensure he hunted you, Hazel, and no one else.'

'You set a demon loose to kill a child,' Titus said, his fingers closing over his pistol.

'I was blinded by grief . . .'

'There are no excuses for what you did!'

'I know,' Lilith said as more tears poured down her face. 'And I'm *sorry.*'

'All right,' Hazel said, pushing Titus a few paces back. 'Just tell us what happened next.'

'Bloodybones shrugged off my magical bonds like an old coat. I knew at once what a terrible mistake I'd made. He drew this circle to imprison me and then did as he pleased. All I could do was wait here and endure my guilt.'

'How did you survive all this time?'

'He returned every now and again to give me food and tell unpalatable stories of the horrible acts he had committed on the streets.' She looked at them with dull eyes. 'So, what are you going to do with me?'

Hazel and Titus exchanged a glance.

'That depends,' Hazel said.

'On what?'

'Well, Frost Witch,' Titus said gravely. 'It depends on whether you want a chance to atone?'

40
DAY OF DAYS

'I will stamp out this foul and noisome
heresy under my boot.'
Witch Hunter Captain John Stearne

The bells of St Paul's chimed seven times as Hazel pelted across London Bridge, dodging early risers and holding her hat on with the flat of her hand.

She and Titus had told Lilith about their desire to rescue the imprisoned witches, and Lilith had needed no convincing to offer her help. Anything, she'd said, to wipe some of the guilt from her conscience.

Then, in private, Hazel and Titus had shared a hurried goodbye. Titus said he'd move heaven and earth to get to the arena in time to travel with her to the Underworld. But Hazel knew it was a vain promise, made by Titus to help him cope with the separation that struck so hard at his heart.

As for her, she'd only just managed to hide her tears from him. She knew it was right for Titus to rescue David and the witches, but leaving him behind was agony. All she could do was vow to find him when she returned from the Underworld with her mother.

'Hazel, slow down,' Bramley said from his nest in her hair. 'I can't sleep with all this bumping around.'

'I can't, I'll be late for duty,' she puffed. 'And I've thought of a problem, but also a way to solve it.'

'What problem?'

Hazel slowed down as she passed through the gate at the north end of the bridge. 'Ah, I thought I saw one here . . . Good, just what I need.'

'*What's* here? Hazel, explain yourself!'

She stepped into a doorway to catch her breath. 'I need some ingredients from in there.'

She nodded across the road to a shop with a sign over the door that read: 'Silvanus Bevan Esq. – Worshipful Society of Apothecaries'. There was movement beyond the stocked window of glass bottles, carafes and fermenters as the owner prepared to open up.

'I need to make sure that Murrell has enough time to recite the spell before his pyre is ignited, right?' Hazel continued.

'Right. He can't open a demon gate if he's on fire.'

'But I *also* want to spare Anthony the task of putting the torch to the pyre. So, two birds, one stone.'

'Aha! So you're going to replace Anthony as the boy who sets the fire, then you can ensure that Murrell has time to say the spell.'

'Exactly.'

'But Hopkins is adamant that he wants Anthony to do it, so how are you going to change his mind?'

'Ah, well, that's why I need to see the apothecary . . .'

222

After purchasing what she needed Hazel knocked on Anthony's bedroom door in the Tower, hoping he had not yet reported for duty. Bramley hid in her hair.

On the second knock the door opened a crack and Anthony, with his hair sticking up as if he'd just crawled out of bed, peered out. 'Hello, William. Is everything all right?' His eyes widened with alarm. 'Am I late? Is the General angry?'

'No, we've a while before we're due on duty,' Hazel replied. 'Can I come in?'

She watched with concern as Anthony perched on the edge of his rumpled bed. He looked distracted and his eyes were red.

Damn Hopkins for putting him through this misery, she thought. *Still, at least I can do something about it.*

'I was hoping the night would last forever,' Anthony said. 'But it didn't, and tonight I've got to . . .'

'Listen to me,' Hazel said. 'I've thought of a way to get you out of lighting the pyre, but –' she scrunched up her face – 'it's a little drastic.'

'I'll do anything,' he said, eyes lighting up. 'Just tell me.'

'Well, the only excuse I can think of that Hopkins will accept is if you get sick. *Really* sick. Sick enough that you have to stay in bed.'

'But I'm not sick, and I don't think I can pretend well enough to fool anyone for long.'

'You won't have to.' Hazel took a paper wrap from

her pocket. 'Not if you eat this.'

Anthony leaned closer. 'What is it?'

Hazel opened the wrap to reveal a few pinches of bitter-smelling powder. 'It's a mixture of herbs and extracts – I had it made up this morning.' She smiled when she saw Anthony's look of surprise. 'My mother is a herbalist, and she taught me some recipes.'

'And it will make me sick?'

'Oh yes, all *over* the place, but only for a day or two and it won't do any lasting damage, I promise. I know it's horrible but it'll get you out of tonight. And the General can't very well blame you for being ill, can he?'

'No, I suppose not.' Anthony looked thoughtful, then nodded his head. 'I'll do it.'

Hazel folded up the wrap and put it in his hand. 'Mix it into your breakfast porridge and eat it all – you'll feel the effects quickly. The General's physician will no doubt send you straight back to bed and you can concentrate on getting better.' She smiled. 'But not until *after* the Pageant, eh?'

Anthony leaped forward and wrapped her in a grateful hug, forcing Bramley to retreat deeper into Hazel's hair. 'Thank you, William!' he cried. 'Oh, I was *so* dreading tonight.'

'That's all right. I'm just sorry I couldn't think of a nicer solution,' Hazel said as Antony let her go. 'So, what are you going to do after this is over? Do you think you'll stay working for the General?'

'I don't like all the things that happen here, so I think

I'll go back home as soon as I'm able,' Anthony said with a shake of his head. 'The General only really wanted me for this one job at the execution, so he won't care if I go.'

'I think you're very wise. We'd better go down to breakfast. I'll stay with you until the powder takes effect and then go and tell the General.'

'Sick?' Hopkins looked up from the paper-strewn desk in his office. 'What do you mean, sick?'

The Witch Hunter General looked exhausted and Hazel suspected that like her he hadn't been to bed. Everyone was preparing for the Execution Pageant, and there was an atmosphere of feverish activity throughout the Tower.

'At breakfast,' Hazel said. 'He looked very pale, said he wasn't feeling well and then, all of a sudden . . .' She mimed someone throwing up.

'Well, how bad is it? Will he be fit for tonight?'

'The physician said no, and that he'd never seen anyone so green.'

Hopkins lowered his head and went very quiet. Hazel braced herself for an explosion, but after a few moments he regained his composure and looked up at her. 'Will the boy be all right?'

'I think so. It was probably something he ate.'

'Well, that's good,' Hopkins muttered, getting up and gazing out of the window. 'Still, it couldn't have come at a worse time. I had wanted him to set light to Murrell's pyre, you know. I thought it would send a message to our enemies that even children are fighting for the Order's cause.'

'Go on, ask him now,' Bramley whispered. 'Ask if you can set the pyre alight.'

But Hazel wanted to pick the right moment. 'Has there been any news about Lord Cromwell?' she asked instead.

'What?' Hopkins said, turning from the window. 'Oh, yes. We've had a message saying he's returned to camp. He'd strayed into enemy territory and had to lie low for a while, but he's quite well. It's a great relief – his loss would be a bitter blow to our struggle against the witch rebellion. Such things put life's smaller problems into perspective.'

'Like Anthony not being able to set light to the pyre tonight,' Hazel said.

'Indeed, although we do need to find a suitable replacement to perform that duty.' Hopkins looked thoughfully at Hazel.

'General?' Hazel kept her expression as bland as possible.

'How about *you*, William?' Hopkins said, circling her. 'Would you like to perform this honourable task in front of the great and good of London tonight? I think you'd be perfect!'

'Me? Really?' Her bland look transformed to one of joy. 'I would be proud to carry out this duty. Thank you, General, for this great honour.'

'Good. That's settled then. Now listen carefully – this is what you'll need to do . . .'

41

THE EXECUTION ARENA

'Can I be blamed for my natural state?
Have I been guilty since birth?'
Maret Jonsdotter's last words before her execution

Titus put the cloth-covered bucket of demon blood on the ground and shook out his aching arm. Tower Hill bustled with people gathering early for the Execution Pageant. That was good – it meant no one was taking any notice of him or Lilith, or the pungent smell of sour milk coming from the bucket.

'It's like a goddamned carnival,' he muttered.

Tower Hill's grassy slopes were already covered in market stalls and brightly coloured pavilions. Hot food vendors, pint-of-ale sellers, coffee pourers and pamphleteers had all staked claim to prime patches and were busily setting up in time for the evening crowd.

At the crest of the hill stood the execution arena. With its twenty-foot walls, corner towers and double-gates, it looked like a miniature fortress. The timbers were stained an appropriate red, and dozens of the Order's crossed-hammer banners hung from the battlements.

Lilith, who had been lagging behind with Hazel's bag

227

of provisions over her shoulder, caught up with Titus and surveyed the activity with a look of disgust on her face. 'Look at these vultures. All seeking to profit from the death of a great man like Nicolas.'

That morning Titus had brought Lilith a pair of boots, a modest blue dress, a lace cap, and a decent breakfast in a chophouse on London Bridge. Now she looked more like the strong, proud witch who had fought as part of Murrell's Coven of rebels.

'Not to mention your fellow witches trapped in the hulk down there,' Titus said, pointing in the direction they'd come. 'Look – they're moving them.'

From their vantage point between the bone-white pile of the Tower on the left and a line of grand houses on the right, was a clear view of the river. Sailors in four rowboats strained at their oars to haul the prison hulk towards a pontoon anchored a quarter of a mile downriver from London Bridge.

Even from this distance Titus saw that the hulk had been covered with flammable pitch. A couple of flaming arrows shot from Cromwell Island would quickly turn it into an inferno – certain death for all those trapped below.

'If we're going to think of a plan to rescue them we'll need a closer look at that pontoon,' he began, before noticing that Lilith was not listening.

She stared at the hulk, arms rigid at her sides, hands balled into fists. Fury came off her in icy waves. Frost crackled across her skin.

Titus sidled up to her. 'Careful, witch, we can't help them from a prison cell.'

Lilith's frost-magic melted away, but her face remained hard and cold. 'So what *are* we going to do?'

'The Witch Hunter guards will abandon the hulk long before they set it ablaze, so getting on board should be easy if we can steal a boat,' Titus said, stroking his beard. 'The problem is how to get over three hundred people off without anyone noticing.'

'We need to think of a way, and quickly,' Lilith replied. 'If I save them from death, perhaps I might find some peace for what I brought down on those children.'

'We're not doing this to salve your conscience – and you'll never be able to make up for what you did.'

'I know, but I—'

'But nothing!' Titus growled. 'You tried to kill Hazel, a *child*! Believe me, if we survive this dreadful night, you and I will have a reckoning.' He picked up the bucket. 'But first things first – the magic circle.'

They made their way through the crowd until they reached the arena. One of the gate doors was open, affording a glimpse inside of tiered seats and a raised wooden platform in the middle. Titus was glad to see a small army of people cleaning, decorating and carrying out repairs in readiness for the night's event.

In all this confusion it should be easy enough to get inside and under the platform without anyone noticing, he thought, checking to ensure the page of the

Necronomicon was safe in his pocket.

'Right,' he said. 'This may take me a while. In the meantime, you need to scout out the hulk and then find us a boat. I'll meet you back at the warehouse this evening.'

Lilith drew Titus behind a parked wagon. 'It's not going to be difficult getting all those prisoners off the hulk – it's going to be impossible. One boatload, *maybe*, before we're spotted.'

'You agreed to help . . .'

'And I'm going to, so listen. If we want to save all the prisoners we can't attempt to get them off the hulk – that's doomed to fail. Instead, we move the hulk with the prisoners still on board.'

'Move the hulk . . . ?'

'We wait for dark, row out, climb on board, then cut the mooring ropes. The river will carry the hulk out of London. We won't be able to steer, but as soon as we run aground we get everyone off.'

Titus thought about it for a few moments. 'And with the Pageant in full swing any pursuit by the Order will be hampered.'

'It could work, couldn't it?' Lilith said, her eyes hopeful.

'Wait though . . . The hulk can still burn. The Order's marksmen on the Island will easily hit it with their fire arrows even if it's moving. We'll all be fried together.'

A smile thawed Lilith's pale face. 'Then it's lucky you've got a Frost Witch on your side, isn't it?'

42
THE *ANESIDORA*

It was nine o'clock and dark by the time Titus returned to the warehouse. Drawing the magic circle had taken time and all his concentration, and the constant fear of discovery had reduced his nerves to tatters. But he had escaped unscathed with the circle complete – it was now up to Murrell to open the gate.

Lilith waited for him at the end of the jetty with a dark shawl pulled tight around her shoulders. 'Is it done?'

'Aye, although only time will tell if I got it right. I could hardly see by the end of it.' He rubbed his hands down his face. 'God's bones, I've never felt so tired.'

London Bridge and the riverbanks blazed with torches. Cheerful voices and laughter drifted on the night-time breeze – the Pageant was in full swing as the time for the executions neared.

Titus and Lilith looked at the hulk moored opposite, with its hatches closed and hull stained black with pitch.

'What if people see us?'

'We have to try and stay out of sight,' Titus said, 'and hope that if we're spotted people take us for members of the Order on official business.'

'Very well. There's a rope ladder astern that we can use to get on board,' Lilith said, climbing into a rowboat tied against the jetty. 'Come on, Witch Finder, we'd better get going. They're due to set it aflame within the hour.'

Titus clambered down after her. 'You have the hatchets?'

Lilith tapped a sack at her feet. 'Two.'

'And your magic? Is it waxing strong?'

'The coldest of winter frosts is locked up in my heart,' she said, unlooping the mooring line.

'It had better be, because our lives and theirs depend on it.'

Putting aside all his aches and pains, Titus fitted the oars into the rowlocks and began to pull towards the hulk. It was a warm night and he was soon sweating into his shirt. Gulls circled overhead, calling to each other. Torchlight floated on the river like slicks of gold.

Allowing the tide to carry them downriver, Titus eased the boat behind the hulk and up to the dangling rope ladder. The stern rose over them like a timber cliff, completely blocking their view of London Bridge. Titus secured the boat, then followed Lilith up the ladder.

The hull beams near the waterline were rotten and covered in barnacles, but the rest had been slathered in tacky, stinking pitch. Titus noted the name of the ship carved in capital letters just below the gun hatches.

The Anesidora, he thought. *A fine ship in your day, by the looks of it. Well, I hope to save you from a fiery end tonight.*

Lilith leaned over the rail to help him up, and when he'd clambered on deck his heart was pounding and he could barely catch a breath. Refusing to let it show, he hurried down a short staircase on to the main deck, being careful to stay low.

There was a padlocked hatch near the mainmast; Titus crouched down and pressed his ear to the boards. He heard voices from below, some frightened, some consoling, and many crying piteously.

'Leave the lock to me,' he said to Lilith, taking a leather pouch from his pocket and laying it out in front of him. 'You fire-proof this boat, and then we can cut her loose.'

'Very well.' Lilith straightened up, took a deep breath and closed her eyes. Her hair stiffened. White vapour cascaded from her skin and rolled over the deck in freezing waves. The air turned frigid as a midwinter night. 'You're staring, Witch Finder,' she said, smiling with pale blue lips.

Breath already misting, Titus tore his eyes away and set about picking the lock.

43
THE GRAND PARADE

William, my new apprentice, is brighter that the normal intake.
I enjoy tutoring him in the ways of the Order.
Taken from Matthew Hopkins' diary

For Hazel, the hours leading up to the Execution Pageant were a whirl of frenzied, exhausting activity. Along with an entourage of administrators and officials – all wound tight with nerves – she followed in the wake of the seemingly tireless Hopkins as he oversaw the finishing touches to the night's grisly events.

The Witch Hunter General was in his element: a bundle of controlled energy, his stocky frame bristling with intent, the whirr of his thoughts almost audible. He barked orders, sent messages, twice marched the route to the arena in the blazing midday sun, briefed staff in endless meetings, and inspected the guards' uniforms – he did not stop once, not even to eat.

Yet Hazel still found time to brood, to worry about what lay before her, and to agonize about the danger she had led her friends into. Would Titus finish the magic circle? Would he rescue David and the other prisoners? Or would he be captured and executed alongside them? Would Bramley –

clever, loyal Bramley – end up trapped with her in the Underworld? Held captive? Hurt? Killed?

And would she see her mother's face again? Was her mother even still alive?

All these thoughts churned endlessly through Hazel's mind until she was so anxious she could barely think straight. She'd checked a hundred times that the *Necronomicon* was safely stashed in the back of her trousers. All she could do now was wait . . . and hope.

As the day wore on, Hazel felt her spirit seep away like water through sand. Her only comfort was Bramley, curled up at the base of her neck and doing his best to hearten her with warm waves of magic.

At last, when Hazel was ready to collapse, the frenzy died down, the storm of activity abated. All orders had been relayed, all messages delivered. The hulk was prepared and in position for its immolation. The guests were arriving in the execution arena on Tower Hill, and even now Murrell was being loaded into the wagon that was to take him to his death.

Or possibly his escape, Hazel thought. *But only if the circle is drawn. And if the spell works. And if, heaven forbid, the Order doesn't gag him so he can't speak.*

Finding themselves alone for the first time that day, Hazel and Hopkins climbed the battlements and looked out over Tower Hill. Dusk was falling, but the hundreds of lanterns strung from poles over the milling crowds and market stalls cast a celebratory light over the whole place.

The blunt, red-stained execution arena presided over it all like a bloody tooth.

'Look at all those people,' Hopkins said, waving his hand at the throng. 'Turning out in their thousands for this spectacle of death. It doesn't sit right with me.'

Hazel looked at him, surprised. 'But don't you believe Murrell deserves this fate?'

'Of course I do, but not like this. Not in this ghoulish carnival.'

Hazel rubbed her temples, numb with fatigue and fretfulness. 'So why does Cromwell order it done this way?'

'For good reasons. Tonight, when those people feel the flames of the pyres on their faces they'll be reminded what happens to the enemies of the Order, be they witches or those who harbour them.' Hopkins sighed. 'Cromwell understands that ordinary people need fear to make them shudderingly submissive. He's right, but it saddens me that it has to be this way.'

He pulled his uniform straight and smiled at her. 'Still, when the rebellion is crushed and our land is finally free of witch-filth we won't have any more need of such demonstrations. And I'll be able to retire to a quiet place with my memories and the knowledge of a job well done.'

Hazel hid her anger behind an expression of polite interest as Hopkins led her to the battlements overlooking the river. From there she saw Cromwell Island and the prison hulk moored against its floating pontoon. People lined the bridge and banks in cheerful expectation.

'Ah, the crowds gather,' Hopkins said. 'And so does my grand parade.'

The embankment was packed with clerks, administrators, Witch Hunters and their apprentices, all looking excited about the coming event. The Grandees gathered in a separate group, all mounted on magnificent warhorses and wearing their best uniforms. Hazel spotted Stearne on his own, hunched morosely over the reins.

'I bet he wants to be in charge of this whole thing,' Bramley whispered. 'He's furious that Hopkins is going to get the credit from Cromwell.'

In the centre of the throng, surrounded by a cordon of immaculately attired soldiers, was the prison wagon – a heavy, four-wheeled cage drawn by two horses. Murrell was inside, filthy, pale, stripped to the waist, with his face hidden behind a curtain of black hair. He looked terrible, but Hazel was relieved to see him ungagged and on his feet.

'We'd better go down,' Hopkins said. 'Remember, you follow the wagon during the parade, but come and stand next to me as soon as we enter the arena. I'll give you the signal and all you need to do is walk up to the pyre and set it alight.'

'Yes, General.' Hazel's voice shook as she contemplated the enormity of what she was about to do. 'I'm ready.'

The air of excitement was thick, and a wave of dizziness overcame Hazel as she crossed the embankment and found her place among the other apprentices behind the wagon. Some looked at her curiously, others stepped away.

I'm the boy who was bewitched, she thought. *No wonder they're nervous.*

The apprentices' reaction gave her a boost of strength, and her fire-magic, which she'd repressed for so long, stirred deep inside. It felt good.

She glanced up at Murrell, who was nearly close enough to touch – but if he saw her he did not acknowledge it, and just stared at something far off in the distance.

I wonder where Thorn is? Hazel thought. *Close by, I'm sure.*

Everyone shuffled into ranks when they saw Hopkins mount his horse at the head of the column. He raised his hand, cried 'Forward!' and the procession began its march to the execution arena.

'Here we go then, Hazel,' Bramley said. 'Once more into the frying pan.'

44
FIRE FROM THE SKY

The scold's bridle – such a marvellous device!
A godsend, you might say.
Methods of Subjugation by Hollis Ertle

Titus blinked the sweat from his eyes and took a deep breath. His back ached from bending over, his shoulders were stiff and, worst of all, his hands were shaking so badly he could hardly fit the lock picks into the padlock. He felt clumsy, unable to *feel* the mechanism in the way he'd done in years gone by.

He glanced up at Cromwell Island and wondered if the archers were already on the roof, preparing their arrows, getting ready to shoot.

A wave of cold air chilled him as a barefoot Lilith drifted past whispering strange words under her breath.

Frost-magic.

Titus had expected ice, pale clouds, eddies of white snow, and feared such visible manifestations would give them away, but the magic Lilith wielded that night was barely visible.

Dark vapour poured from her skin, and on every board, mast and rope it touched there formed crystals shining darkly in the moonlight. Her every footfall left a black ice imprint which seeped into the deck and cracked the wood, leaving it freezing but not slippery to the touch.

The witch is doing her job. I have to do mine, Titus thought.

Pinching the picks between fingers and thumb, he inserted them back into the lock and began to probe. A twist and one of the tumblers inside snapped into position. One more and the lock would spring, freeing David and the witches from their prison.

A drop of sweat trickled down his nose as he tried to get a purchase on the second tumbler. His heart quickened as he felt a click, then the lock mechanism snapped back into place and sent the pick flying into the air.

'God *dammit!*'

Lilith stole up behind him and rested her slender hands on his shoulders. 'Calm yourself, Witch Finder,' she said into his ear. 'You can do this, just have a little faith.'

Frost-magic seeped over him, cooling his anger, smoothing his frustration. He gasped as the sweat on his face froze and then fell away in a cloud of ice vapour. In moments he felt stronger in body and sharper in mind – in fact he felt twenty years younger.

Amazed, he turned round, but Lilith was already gliding towards the bows, leaving a trail of ice behind her.

Titus pulled another pair of picks from the leather pouch and got back to work. Almost immediately he felt a satisfying click, then another, and with a deft twist of his wrist the padlock sprang open.

'Thank God,' he muttered.

When he heaved the hatch open he was met with cries of fear, a wave of heat, and a stench so bad he was forced to cover his nose with the back of his hand.

'It's all right,' he shouted. 'I'm not a Witch Hunter, I'm here to rescue you.'

As his eyes adjusted he saw a mass of filthy upturned faces, all women, with their expressions slowly changing from terror to hope.

'Pass down a ladder,' one cried. 'We must get out of here before it goes up in flames.'

'We have sick people down here . . . Can they be helped too?'

'Is this a trick? Who *are* you?'

'Please, calm yourselves,' Titus said, but the clamour of voices just got louder.

'Ladies, for pity's sake be quiet and let the man speak.' A stout, middle-aged woman with a Scottish brogue forced her way through the press and peered up at Titus. 'I think you'd better explain who you are, sir, and exactly what it is you intend to do.'

'My name is Titus White, and I . . .' He thought for a moment and then said, 'I'm working for the rebellion. Not directly, but I share their desire to disrupt the Order in any way possible.'

The clamour from the hulk quietened, and he heard his

words being passed deeper into the ship from one captive to another.

'I'm here with a Wielder, a Frost Witch who is also a friend to the rebellion,' he continued. 'We want to help every one of you, but we can't get you off the hulk right now. You understand? We're in the middle of London and we only have one rowboat.'

'So what's the plan?' the Scottish witch asked.

'We're going to unmoor this hell-ship and let the tide pull it out of the city. You can come up on deck then, and when it runs aground you can disembark and lose yourselves in the countryside. I can't guarantee success, but at the least it's a chance of escape.'

There was a stunned silence, and then the Scottish witch grinned. 'Well, I can't speak for my fellow prisoners, but I approve mightily.'

'I'm glad to hear it,' Titus said, returning her smile. 'Because it's the only plan we have.'

'My name's Vida, Mr White,' the Scottish witch said. 'What can we do to help?'

'Are any of you chained up, or locked in cells?'

'No, but most of us haven't eaten much for days, and some are very sick.' Vida frowned. 'I can organize the strongest of us into groups to help those who need it. We'll all stick together, Mr White. It's the only way.'

'Good idea.' Titus decided he liked Vida and knew that with her help their chances of success had increased.

The prisoners with a view of the hatch gasped as Lilith,

her face smooth and white as driven snow and her hair frosted with magic, appeared at Titus's side. 'It's nearly time,' she said, handing Titus one of the hatchets. 'The arrows will be falling soon. We must be quick.'

Titus nodded, then leaned down towards Vida. 'Listen, is there a boy down there with you? Tall, dark hair, goes by the name of David?'

'The one-eyed lad?' Vida said. 'Why, yes. The Witch Hunters threw him down here the other day. Is he known to you?'

Titus closed his eyes as a flood of relief engulfed him. 'Yes, yes he is. He was my apprentice. Is he hurt?'

'No, but he's hardly said a word since he arrived. We've done our best to comfort him, although until you turned up we've had precious little hope to quell his fears.' She frowned. 'Does that mean the dog is yours too?'

Titus looked at her blankly. 'Dog?'

'The boy came with a dog, a great slobbery hound. Won't leave his side.'

Despite the peril, Titus smiled. 'That sounds like my Samson. You are truly the bearer of good news, Vida.'

'Titus,' Lilith said. 'Enough talk. Time to *go*.' She pointed to the top of Cromwell Island as the first fire arrows traced orange arcs on to the sky and began to plummet towards them.

45
INTO THE ARENA

In the night sky I saw them, cutting across the moon on their besoms. Witches – a devil's dozen. 'Flee!' I cried. And we did.
Memoirs of an Innkeeper by Timothy Taylor

The column marched up the hill between two lines of yelling spectators, men, women and even children all hurling abuse at the caged Murrell. Hazel had expected it, but the naked aggression on their faces shocked her. How could anyone feel such hatred for another person? Especially one who was being taken to his death?

Bramley stirred nervously behind her ear, and Hazel had to resist the urge to reach up and touch him.

'These people hardly think of Murrell as human any more, not after all the terrible things the Order has said about him,' he said.

The wagon creaked round a bend, affording a view of Hopkins at the head of the column. A few people cheered and waved to him but most focused on the wagon.

'I never thought I'd say this, Hazel,' Bramley said, 'but you need to be just like Murrell. Look how composed he is! You'd think he was out for a Sunday stroll.'

The red walls of the execution arena got closer, the

crossed-hammer banners hanging limp in the humid air. There were even more soldiers here, lining the last few yards and struggling to hold the crowd back. Hazel glanced behind, hoping to get a glimpse of the prison hulk, but there was a pint-of-ale pavilion in the way.

What time was it? When were the fire arrows due to fall? Was Titus on board? Was Lilith doing as she'd promised? David and the prisoners – would they live this night, or die in the most horrible way imaginable?

Through the gates she marched, glad to leave the crowds behind. *I must be calm. Think about what you can control, and forget everything else. Wait for Murrell . . . Gate opens . . . Walk in. That's it.*

Despite being open to the sky, the arena felt hotter and the air harder to breathe. A packed audience sat in a steeply tiered circle of seats, segregated by class and social status.

Periwigged lords and silk-clad ladies fanned themselves with pamphlets; Guild Masters (including the Master of the Plague Doctors wearing a big hat that he hoped would hide him from 'Hopkins' brother') with crests proudly adorned on their chests; infantry officers and their more flamboyant cavalry counterparts, and grim-faced, black-clad Witch Hunters.

Hazel thought there must be at least two hundred people packed inside – the great and good of London and beyond, descended here to witness what they hoped would be the violent end of Nicolas Murrell, feared demonologist and arch-enemy of England.

Or so they think, she thought. *Whatever happens, none of them will forget what they're about to witness.*

A heavy timber platform nearly as tall as Hazel dominated the centre of the arena; it was usually used for hangings, but the gallows had been removed and a roofless iron cage with a gate had been constructed around it. Inside was a thick layer of pitch-covered straw and kindling, supporting wooden planks sturdy enough to stand on. There was no stake for Murrell to be tied to.

It's like he's going to die on stage, Hazel realized with horror. *Perhaps they want to see him run around, try to climb out, cling to the bars and beg for release*. The cruelty of it took her breath away.

A flurry of gasps and excited whispers echoed around the arena as the wagon drew to a halt and the audience caught their first glimpse of the prisoner.

The Grandees dismounted, handed the reins to waiting grooms and found their places in a block of reserved seats behind a raised lectern. The rest of the column dispersed into the tiers, and the soldiers spaced themselves around the outside the platform. After the grooms had taken the horses from the arena the guards closed and barred the gates, blocking the sound of the baying crowd.

Hazel looked round for Hopkins and saw him dismount and stride up to the lectern.

'You'd better go and join him,' Bramley whispered. 'It's time to find out if this insane plan of yours is going to work.'

246

46
COLD DECEPTION

I drank the witch's brew, and lo! My ailment
was cured and I felt my youth return to me!
In Excelsis *by William Kerr*

Lilith stepped behind the mast as the first arrows struck. Many fell short and disappeared into the Thames, but some reached the hulk, bouncing off the yardarms and thwacking into the deck. The archers were finding their range and Titus knew that the next volley would be more accurate.

He scrambled behind an empty cannon carriage, wincing as one of the spluttering missiles embedded itself in the timber with a thump. Keeping his head down, he called down the hatch to the prisoners.

'They've started,' he said over their cries. 'I'm going to close the hatch to keep you safe, and then cut the mooring lines. Do you understand?'

'Aye, Mr White, off you go – I'll sort out this rabble,' Vida called. 'Now come on, sisters, we must stay calm . . .'

There were two ropes securing the hulk to the pontoon, one at the stern, one at the bow. Titus hefted his hatchet and examined the blade, deciding a few heavy,

247

well-aimed strikes should do the trick.

Assuming I don't get skewered first, he thought, hearing a cheer rise from the riverbanks as another dozen arrows skittered across the deck. *And it won't be long before people wonder why the hulk isn't catching fire.*

He peered out from behind the gun carriage to judge the distance to the stern rope and what cover he could use to shelter from the arrows. His eyes widened as pale yellow flames spread across the deck, licking up the rigging and rope-lines. Smoke eddies drifted over him, catching in his throat.

'What the *hell?*' He rounded on Lilith and found her smiling at him. 'The fire – it's taking hold. Why isn't your magic working?'

'My magic is working in precisely the way I intend.'

'Then why does the ship burn?' Titus raged. 'Have you betrayed us, witch?'

Lilith shook her head. 'The fire you see is real and will spread and dance as fire should. But my frost-magic is stronger and steals all its heat and destructiveness. Do not fear – no harm will come to us, even if we walk right through it.'

Titus stared at her in growing wonder. 'So from the banks it will look as if all is going as expected . . . There'll be no pursuit?'

'Correct. And when the hulk starts to move downriver they'll assume the fire has burned through the ropes and watch us drift away.' Lilith smiled as she lifted her hatchet. 'So, to work, Witch Finder – it's time to make our escape.'

Keeping out of sight below the gunwale, Titus made his way towards the rear of the hulk and the steps leading up to the quarterdeck. He ducked as another volley of arrows hissed and clattered overhead, falling like comets through the spars and yardarms.

The fire spread with terrifying speed, spilling like liquid across the decks in all directions, and then whirling up the masts and along the ratlines. Flickering orange light bathed everything, and over Titus's head rose a roiling column of smoke. Fed by the breeze, the fire was turning into an inferno.

Titus held up his hands to protect himself from the glare, yet he felt no heat and it was to his amazement that in the heart of the fire's rage, under the crackle and roar, the surfaces it touched – wood, rope or canvas – remained undamaged.

I've seen some sights in my time, but nothing matches this.

Lilith was already hacking away at the bow so he clambered up the stairs on to the quarterdeck. The mooring line, thick as a man's wrist and encrusted with black ice, had been looped through a heavy iron ring mounted on the deck.

Titus took aim and swung the hatchet. The blow shivered up his arm, but his blood was up and with a few more powerful strokes he split the line in a blizzard of ice and rope fibres. The frayed end slipped through the ring and over the side.

Done. They were free on the pontoon. Now it was all up to the river.

He peered over the gunwale at the swollen hull of the ship. At first nothing happened and Titus wondered if there was another rope to cut, then the gap between boat and pontoon began to widen. One foot . . . two . . . until a black gulf opened with a glimpse of gold-flecked water far below. With an inevitability that still seemed miraculous, the creaking old hulk started to slide away from the pontoon.

Titus felt the light sway of the hulk's deck and a groan from the rotten timbers deep in her hull: after so many years shackled to a jetty, the *Anesidora* was making her final voyage, wreathed in flames and carrying a cargo of rescued witches.

'I hate to tempt the fates but I think we've got away with it,' he said as Lilith glided up the steps and crouched next to him. 'The dolts onshore have no idea what's really happening!'

The Wielder nodded as a wave of fire swept over the quarterdeck and engulfed them in a kaleidoscope of shimmering light. 'Yes, we've done well, you and I, but I fear this is just the beginning.'

'There's always another battle to be fought, but it's important to appreciate the victories before buckling on the sword belt again.'

They were already drifting past Cromwell Island and

beyond the city walls. The *Anesidora* was unsteered and listing, but for the time being she kept to the middle of the river. With a tail-wind of luck they'd make it a few miles out of London before she beached.

Lilith watched Titus carefully, then she slipped her hand in his pocket and pulled out his watch. 'It's an hour before Nicolas is due to be executed. You still have time – she need not go to the Underworld alone.'

'How did you know I was thinking about Hazel?'

'What an absurd question,' Lilith said, helping Titus to his feet. 'You and that girl may as well be family. Now go.'

'But what about . . . ?'

'I'll take care of the prisoners. Now, take the rowboat and get to Tower Hill – you can make it, but only if you leave now.'

'Are you sure?'

'I'm sure. It's my job to get my sisters to safety. It's yours to be with your witch.'

They walked together to the rope ladder.

'I don't know if anything you do will make up for the deaths of those girls, Lilith,' Titus said. 'But I believe you're going to try.'

'I am,' she said quietly. 'With all my heart.'

Titus put his foot on the first rung. 'I'm trusting you to put aside our differences and look after David for me. *And* my dog. Will you do that?'

'If they'll let me.'

'And tell David . . . Tell him he's got nothing to feel

251

guilty about.' Titus chewed his lip. 'Tell him if we meet again it'll be me asking for *his* forgiveness.'

'He'll know what that means?'

Titus nodded 'What will you do when this heap beaches?'

'We won't be safe from the Order in the South, so I'll take as many of my sisters as I can to the North and meet up with the rebels.'

'A sound plan. Tread softly, and stay off the main highways. It's a long and dangerous journey.'

Lilith arched an eyebrow. 'I didn't come down in the last rainstorm, Witch Finder.'

'Snowstorm, surely?'

Her face melted into a smile. 'Assuming you survive whatever lies ahead, how do you expect to find us again?'

'A Frost Witch, a one-eyed boy and a giant hound all fighting for the rebellion?' Titus grinned and began to climb down to the rowboat. 'I'm sure you won't be too hard to track down.'

'Goodbye, Titus,' Lilith called. 'Until we meet again.'

47
THE PYRE

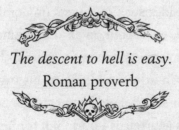

The descent to hell is easy.
Roman proverb

Hazel walked around the edge of the seats, feeling horribly conspicuous, despite the fact that everyone's attention was on Murrell as two soldiers opened the wagon and dragged him out.

Hopkins gave her an encouraging smile as she took up position next to him. 'When I give you the signal, use one of those torches to set light to the straw at the base of the pyre, then step well back. Ready?'

Feeling very unready, Hazel nodded.

'Good lad.'

Hopkins mounted the steps and grasped the lectern with both hands. An expectant hush fell as he cast his gaze around the auditorium.

'Friends, comrades, I bid you welcome,' he said, his strident voice carrying to every corner.' You are about to witness a truly historic event. For tonight we serve justice. Tonight our greatest enemy passes from this world . . . into *oblivion.*'

There was a scattering of applause from some of the lords and ladies in the top tiers, but most of the audience seemed to consider such outbursts unseemly. Instead they leaned forward, eyes fixed on an unresisting Murrell as he was marched up some steps to the gate in the cage.

'Behold the murderer walking to his own termination,' Hopkins continued. 'Behold the necromancer facing death. Behold Nicolas Murrell as I burn him for his sins.'

More applause this time and a few cries of 'Roast him!' The Grandees remained impassive, all except Stearne, who was glaring intently at the back of Hopkins' head.

The soldiers thrust Murrell into the cage, slammed the door and locked it. Standing straight, Murrell faced Hopkins with the corners of his mouth turned up into a smile.

Hazel sensed the audience's unease; this was not what they had expected. Where was the man broken by the administrations of the Order? Where was the man facing death with a scream? They felt cheated, robbed of the spectacle that had been promised – and Hopkins knew it.

'Do not be fooled by this show of indifference,' he said. 'It's just another lie – inside, this man's soul quakes with fear!'

It occurred to Hazel that there was nothing to stop Murrell from reciting the spell right now. She knew the moment would soon come when she'd be ordered to set the fire, so why was the demonologist hesitating?

Do it! she willed him. *Do it now before it's too late!*

'I decree, in my capacity as the Witch Hunter General,

that Nicolas Murrell be put to death by fire.' Sweat flicked from Hopkins' shiny brow. 'I decree the sentence just, right, and proper. Does the prisoner have anything to say?'

There was absolute silence as Murrell kept his eyes on Hopkins and slowly shook his head.

'No last words? No final insults to throw at we who bested you?' Hopkins said. 'Very well. Then I will waste no more time on you, Nicolas Murrell. It's time for you to meet your end.'

That was Hazel's cue. Feeling the weight of every gaze upon her, she walked stiffly to the nearest torch and picked it up from its sconce. It was heavy, and the crackling flame warmed her face.

The platform was no more than ten paces away, and it would take only moments for the pitch and kindling to catch light and spread. *I can't hesitate much longer,* she thought, feeling panic rise into her throat. *What if he doesn't recite the spell in time?*

Murrell stood in the middle of the cage with his head lowered as if in prayer. Was he speaking the demonic words? She couldn't see his face, and the crowd was getting restive.

'Hazel,' Bramley hissed. 'You can't stand here forever – people are wondering what's wrong with you.'

The sight of earnest, truth-speaking Thorn landing on top of the cage, his red breast shining in the lantern light, made up Hazel's mind: at this moment she had no choice but to trust Murrell to hold true to his word; her fate and that of her mother's was in his hands now.

Holding the torch in both hands, she walked steadily towards the pyre. Each footstep took an age. The air felt thick, something she had to cleave through. Smoke from the torch made her eyes water.

A pitch-soaked taper of straw hung down through the bars of the cage. *That's it. That's where I start the fire.* There was no sign of any magic, no sign of a demon gate appearing. The torch wobbled as Hazel inched it towards the taper. As one, the crowd leaned forward.

Murrell reached up and pushed the hair away from his face. His eyes flashed in the torchlight and to her relief Hazel saw his lips moving, quickly and silently – he was reciting the spell.

She was about to step away and let Murrell finish when he reached through the bars and grabbed her wrist. There was a collective gasp of shock and a few people stood up.

'When the gate opens, run inside and do not look back. I'll follow,' Murrell whispered. Then he snatched the torch from her and bore it aloft into the middle of the cage.

He'll follow? Hazel thought. *Does that mean he's coming too?*

Cries echoed around the arena. The Grandees fidgeted in their seats. Without taking his eyes from Murrell, Stearne spat out a wad of tobacco and wiped his lips on his sleeve.

Hopkins slapped his hand down on the lectern. 'Use another torch, William. Hurry up and get this circus over . . .'

Murrell's cry rent the air, shattering the silence into a

million pieces. His mouth stretched wide, and his spine bent so far back Hazel thought it would snap.

A vibration from deep under the earth shook the platform, making the planks shiver and the bars of the cave quiver like bow strings. Another, which Hazel felt through the soles of her feet, made the tiered seats sway and nails spring from the timber like crossbow bolts.

'It's happening, Hazel,' Bramley squeaked. 'Murrell is opening the gate!'

48
VENGEANCE

Take my bones to the Underworld,
and my soul will follow.
The Baroness by John Dyler Baizley

A column of magic rose up around Murrell, shimmering like water reflecting on glass. Hazel stared in wonder as the demonologist, arms outstretched, was lifted high into the air and over the cage bars. Hopkins, gripping the lectern as if for protection, stared at him in terror. People were screaming, jumping from their seats and heading for the closed gates.

'Now, at the last, I would speak to thee, Witch Butcher!' Magically amplified, Murrell's voice boomed to every corner of the arena. 'And I say this: your blood-stained Order has sewn seeds of hate all across this land. Now it is time to reap the harvest.' He held out the torch and let it fall. 'Behold my vengeance!'

The torch hit the platform, bounced once, then landed on its side. A heartbeat's pause, an air-sucking *whump*, and then the fire was born, raging, crackling, bursting through the cage bars with such ferocity that Hazel was forced to turn her face away.

Panic gripped the arena. Lords, ladies, Guild Masters and soldiers fell over each other to reach the gate, scrambling across seats, stumbling and falling in a mad dash. Seeing the advancing exodus, the guards opened the gates and fled. Like the narrow pupil in an eye of fire, Murrell floated higher, his black hair waving around his face. Only Stearne kept his head, gathering a group of his bravest soldiers to shoot up at him, but whether it was through bad aim or the effects of the magic, the bullets went wide.

Hazel didn't want anyone hurt, but a part of her was glad that these allies of the Order were getting a taste of fear. *Now they know what it's like for us witches.*

The ground lurched again, violent enough this time to throw people off their feet. A rumbling noise like an avalanche of stone drowned out all other sound and then the blazing pyre – wood, straw and cage – was swallowed up.

Through the smoke and swirling magic Hazel saw a gaping hole where the pyre had stood just a moment ago, and a stone passage choked with stalactites leading steeply down into darkness.

The demon gate was open.

'I'm going in, Bram,' Hazel said, her voice shaking.

'Come on then, my little witch.' Bramley's heart beat fast against her neck. 'Quickly now.'

A calm feeling of resolve fell over Hazel as she examined the yawning gate between worlds. Black smoke curled out,

259

and the floor was littered with smouldering pieces of the platform. But before she could take a single step someone grabbed her arm and pulled her backwards. It was Hopkins, his soft face white with terror.

'William,' he breathed. 'Don't go any closer – who knows where that portal leads? Stay close to me and I'll make sure . . .' His gaze strayed over her shoulder towards the passage. The corners of his mouth turned down. He began to tremble. 'Oh God, what has he done? What has that maniac *done*?'

The column of magic set Murrell by the lectern. A grin slashed across his face. 'I told you, Witch Butcher, I bring *vengeance*. Vengeance upon you and your Order.'

Hazel followed Hopkins' stare and saw something emerging from the smoke-filled passage. Wolf-like, it loped on clawed feet. Its eyeless head was low to the ground, as if following a scent, and as it got closer Hazel caught a coppery scent, like warm blood.

Bramley quailed behind her ear. 'I think that's . . . Rawhead.'

Cold horror flooded Hazel's veins. So *this* was the shape of Murrell's vengeance: his pet demon summoned once again from the Underworld and set loose on Hopkins and the Order. The magic around the circle began to lash and flicker like whips of lightning. Thorn took to the air and disappeared into the night sky.

Murrell watched him go, a flicker of sadness on his face, then he turned back to Hazel. 'You have a minute before the gate closes,' he cried. 'No innocents will die – Rawhead is only interested in Hopkins and his men. You have my word on that.'

Hopkins backed away and started to run towards his horse, which reared and shied near the wall. Most of the Witch Hunters and Grandees had already fled, joining the crush to get out. The Spymaster remained in his seat, gasping for air with one hand clutching his heart.

Eschewing escape, Stearne had positioned himself halfway up the auditorium, cajoling his soldiers into a line overlooking the passage. 'Steady, boys,' Hazel heard him yell. 'Wait for my order to shoot . . .'

Having faced Rawhead before, Hazel knew he was a lethal predator. Men would die, of that she was sure. *I could stay here and help them fight.*

Then she thought of the inmates of Cromwell Island, bound in chains and misery, their lives stolen; she thought of the countless executions, the women condemned inside the prison hulk, the shadow of the gallows that fell over the whole land; Hazel thought of those things and decided she didn't care what horrible fate awaited Hopkins and his henchmen.

Rawhead emerged from the cave, his greasy skin shining in the scattered fires. He sniffed the air and slinked after Hopkins, teeth-lined jaws agape.

'Go, Hazel!' Murrell cried. 'Abandon these butchers to their fate.'

'Hazel?' Bramley whispered. 'Are you really going to

leave them here with that . . . thing?'

Hazel's heart turned flint-hard as she turned her face from the world.

Ma, she thought, and strode into the cave.

49
A MAN ALONE

As a child he took affright at an apparition of a demon
under his bed: a grey thing like a dog but thrice as big.
The Life and Death of Matthew Hopkins by Andrew Flint

Titus fought his way up Tower Hill, past the fleeing, screaming crowd, chest heaving, heart labouring. Not for a moment did he slow down. He would accompany that foolish girl into the Underworld or he'd be *damned*.

Damned? he thought. *Huh! Damned is right.*

Ahead, between the abandoned pavilions and half-trampled market stalls, stood the execution arena. People poured from the gates – Witch Hunters, apprentices, finely dressed ladies and gentlemen – all casting terrified looks over their shoulders. Others scrambled over the battlements, using the Order banners hanging from the walls to half climb, half slide to the ground.

Titus gritted his teeth and put on another burst of speed; the portal to the Underworld was clearly open, which meant that Hazel was probably already inside. He had to hurry.

Gusts of smoke wafted through the arena gate, heavy with sulphur. Wiping his streaming eyes, Titus entered. So thick was the smoke, and so desperate was he to reach the portal before it closed, that he didn't see the horse and rider barrelling towards him until it was almost too late. He dived out of the way just in time and watched it pelt down the hill.

Was that Hopkins? he wondered. And who was the boy in the apprentice's uniform slumped over the saddle in a dead faint? Not Hazel – the hair was too short. Hopkins must be rescuing him from whatever danger awaited within. He pressed on into the arena.

'Hazel!' he bellowed. '*Hazel!*'

Pressing his sleeve against his nose and mouth, he edged around the rows of empty seats. The smoke cleared a little and he saw that the platform under which he had painted the magic circle had been replaced with a glowing hole in the ground.

The gate *was* open!

Trying to ignore the pain jabbing into his heart, Titus skirted closer towards the edge and saw the mouth of a passage leading down. From it issued a deep rumbling sound, so low as to be almost beyond his hearing. A scene of death and devastation lay all around, shocking even to a hardened Witch Finder like Titus.

A soldier lay spread-eagled on his back, breastplate dented, eyes staring blindly at the sky; a man whom Titus recognized from the castle as Grimstone was bent head first over some seats, blood clotting on his fur robes; an ancient Grandee sat in the front row, hand on heart, face frozen in death.

What the hell had happened here? And where was Hazel? Titus's legs buckled and he collapsed to his knees as he thought of her lying dead in all this carnage. *No, she's alive – I feel it in my bones*, he told himself. *Get up, old man, and go to her*. Slowly, painfully, he clambered to his feet, and when he did he saw that at least one man was still alive.

Witch Hunter Captain John Stearne sat propped up against the shattered remains of a lectern. His right arm, gashed from shoulder to elbow, lay useless in his lap. White from blood loss, he was using his good arm to pour gunpowder into a pistol held upright between his legs. He froze as someone screamed from the depths of the smoke. When it cut off, he grimaced and went back to loading his weapon.

Murrell's set a demon loose, Titus thought. *What else could have cut such a swathe through all these men?*

He nearly cried out as Thorn flew out of the sky and landed on his shoulder; the normally calm little bird was fluttering with anxiety.

'Where's Hazel?' Titus said. 'Is she alive? Tell me quickly!'

'Alive, yes,' Thorn replied, twitching unhappily. 'She's already passed into the Underworld.'

'Then I must hurry—'

'Wait! There is danger – Nicolas summoned a demon to lay waste to his enemies.'

'God dammit! So it's just as I thought . . . I knew he'd have his own agenda.'

'He didn't tell me he was going to do such a thing,' Thorn fretted. 'All this death . . .'

'I don't care about the Witch Hunters,' Titus snarled. 'I say they've got what they deserved, but I must get through that gate.' He peered through the smoke, but all he saw were empty seats. 'What manner of demon is it, and where's it hiding? Can I make it without being seen?'

There was movement above him, and when Titus looked up he saw Rawhead balanced on the back of a row of seats, hindquarters quivering like those of a cat preparing to pounce.

'You again!' Titus threw himself to one side as the demon leaped. Claws slashed empty air, jaws snapped shut on nothing.

Titus rolled towards the edge of the circle, hoping to cross the threshold and perhaps escape that way, but Rawhead landed perfectly on all four feet and loped in a circle, cutting him off from the passage entrance. Thorn flew high, wings thrumming, and disappeared into the smoke.

Titus drew deep from his well of strength and turned to face his enemy. He glared at the hideous, eyeless head, the curved teeth, then spat on the ground.

'*That's* what I think of you,' Titus growled, and quicker than a man half his age, he drew his pistol, sighted along the barrel and fired.

The bullet struck Rawhead's shoulder with a meaty thwack and a puff of blood. As the demon staggered, Titus reached for a discarded halberd lying on the ground. He managed to get one hand around the haft and was beginning to swing it to defend himself when, with his clawed feet slashing great welts in the packed-dirt floor, Rawhead struck.

A cry escaped Titus as the demon rammed into his midriff and tossed him up with a jerk of his head. There was a brief moment of weightlessness and then a bone-shaking impact as Titus landed hard in the space between the first two rows of seats. He groaned, bruised and bleeding, scrabbling uselessly, trying to get up. A spear thrust of pain in his side told him he'd broken some ribs.

Yet even through his agony he railed and fumed: this blasted creature had stopped him from reaching the girl. In the end, after every battle and fight, he'd failed. Damn it all, he'd been so *close*!

Two sets of claws hooked over the seats right over where Titus lay, followed by the demon's great, pale head. Purple muscles around the neck contracted as he opened his lethal jaws.

And so my life ends as it began, Titus thought, refusing to look away. *Alone*.

Far above a bird circled. It was Thorn. Titus fixed his eyes on the little familiar and waited for the end.

A wash of orange light swept over him. He gasped as the air turned dry and a second later the world roared and filled with fire. Unable to breathe in the sudden heat, Titus rolled under the seat, protecting the back of his head with clasped hands. His nose filled with the smell of brimstone and roasting meat.

Trapped in the tumult, Titus could only hope for its abatement, and when the wave of fire and fury faded he saw that Rawhead had gone, Thorn had gone, and the star-clad sky was once again black.

He knew what had just happened and who had caused it, and when Hazel's tear-streaked face appeared over him, and he felt her lift his head and cradle it in her arms, he smiled.

Ah, he thought as the world faded away. *Not alone after all.*

50
A NEW BEGINNING

On retirement I shall find a quiet place to reflect
on my life, and those who I loved and lost.
Taken from Matthew Hopkins' diary

'I came back for you, so don't you *dare* leave me now,' Hazel cried. 'Come on, old man, wake *up*!' She took hold of Titus's lapels and shook him, but his eyes remained shut and when his head lolled back she saw blood crusting on his hairline.

'Is he breathing?' Bramley squeaked, clinging on to her ear.

'I think so,' Thorn said from Hazel's other shoulder. 'We need to wake him and get out of here before this fire gets any worse.'

He was right – fed by a growing breeze, the fire Hazel had cast to kill Rawhead was spreading across the arena, throwing more smoke and sparks into the sky. Soon the whole place would be ablaze.

Hazel swept the tears from her eyes and rummaged in Titus's pockets until she found his pipe pouch. Taking out a pinch of tobacco, she held it under his nose and rubbed the leaves between her fingers to release their sweet smell.

Bramley and Thorn watched, quietly hoping for the best.

Titus's nose twitched, then he sniffed so hard he inhaled a few tobacco leaves. 'Oh, my back, my *head...*' he groaned, opening his eyes and slowly focusing on Hazel. 'What's going on?'

'I'm rescuing you, that's what's going on,' Hazel said, her face breaking into a smile of relief.

'We must go, Titus White,' Thorn said. 'The Order will venture back here any moment.'

'Is the gate to the Underworld still open?' Titus asked, struggling to sit up. 'Is there still time?'

Hazel shook her head, biting her lip as she hoisted his arm over her shoulder and helped him to his feet. 'No.'

Titus stared at her. 'It . . . closed?'

'Murrell said it would only stay open for a short while.' She nodded to the ground in the centre of the arena – all that remained of the gate was the scorched outline of Titus's magic circle.

'But you were already through,' Titus said, shaking his head as if trying to clear it. 'You were on your way . . .'

'Thorn found me and said you were facing Rawhead alone. So I came back.'

'But Hazel – your *mother.*'

She looked away, but Titus could see the gleam of fierce tears in her eyes. 'I know.'

With Hazel taking Titus's weight, they stumbled outside. A few people were cautiously approaching, their faces bathed in firelight. Most of the arena was now ablaze.

A banner caught light, burned free from its moorings and corkscrewed into the air.

'We'd better make ourselves scarce,' Bramley said.

Thorn flew into the air and circled over their heads. 'The mouse is right. There are soldiers and Witch Hunters heading this way from the Tower.'

They picked their way through the market stalls as fast as they could, feeling the heat slowly fade from their backs. Titus winced with every shuffled step.

'We need to find you a doctor,' Hazel said.

'I'm all right. A few broken ribs – I've had worse.'

'A few minutes ago we thought you were *dead*,' Bramley squeaked.

'I'm all right.' Titus removed his arm from Hazel's shoulder and took a few experimental steps. 'See?'

They entered a quiet street leading down to the river. Breathing hard, Titus held up his hand for them to stop.

'You shouldn't have come back,' he said, leaning against a wall.

'Titus . . .' Hazel sighed.

'After everything we'd been through to open that damned gate, you abandon your search –' he jabbed his finger into his chest – 'for me?'

'Oh, you are so stupid sometimes!' The street glowed as Hazel emitted a flash of magic. 'Of course I came back. Don't you know what you *are* to me, Titus?'

'What I am?'

'I love my mother with all my heart, and I'll do anything

to get her back.' Hazel closed her eyes and let her magic fade away. 'Anything except leave my friends to die.'

Titus's anger dissipated. 'It was still a stupid thing to do . . .'

'I know,' Hazel said, letting the tears fall down her cheeks. 'But here we are.'

She slipped her arm into Titus's and together they carried on towards the river, seeing the sky over the rooftops beginning to lighten.

Titus frowned as Thorn landed on his shoulder. 'And what do you think you're doing?'

'I'm tired, Titus White,' he chirruped. 'I need somewhere to rest.'

'All right, you can stay there for a little while,' the old Witch Finder grumbled, 'as long as you don't make any noise.'

'I won't,' Thorn said, settling down on his one good leg. 'I rarely speak unless absolutely necessary.'

'So what are we to do now?' Bramley said. 'We've got this far and ended up right where we started.'

'Not quite,' Hazel said. 'We have the *Necronomicon* so we can still open a gate to the Underworld.'

'But what about the demon blood we need?' Thorn asked. 'And who will recite the spell?'

'I would think that if there are any Wielders or demonologists left in England who can help us, they'll be fighting Cromwell in the North.' Hazel looked up at Titus. 'What do you think, old man?'

'Join up with the rebels, eh?' Titus murmured. 'There's a notion. We're certainly not safe in London, and I for one would be glad to help anyone who's kicking back against the Order.'

'And if we did find someone to help us open another gate,' Bramley said, 'we'd be able to prepare for the journey beforehand, and not just run blindly in and hope for the best.'

'North is where Lilith is going too,' Titus added, 'along with any of the prisoners willing to join her.'

'Oh, of course!' Hazel cried, brushing her sleeve over her face and leaving sooty streaks behind. 'After everything that's happened I nearly forgot about the prisoners. What happened? Did you save them from the fire?'

'We did, and gave them at least a fighting chance of escape.'

'And David?' Hazel said. 'Was he there too?'

'He was, thank God, although I didn't get to see him. I still hope for reconciliation.'

'Me too,' Hazel said quietly. 'Me too.'

They reached the bottom of the street and turned right on the embankment towards London Bridge.

'Oh, but here's something to cheer us up,' Titus said. 'Samson is alive and well and looking after David.'

'He is?' Hazel smiled. 'Now that *is* good news.'

Thorn took off and landed next to Bramley on Hazel's head. 'Who's Samson?'

'Samson is a smelly, slobbery hound,' Bramley declared,

273

'with little in the way of intelligence.'

'It's a shame you think that about my dog, Master Mouse,' Titus said. 'Because he's only got nice things to say about you.'

Hazel glanced back as they passed through the gate and on to London Bridge. She wouldn't miss the city, and was glad to be leaving the Tower and the Island behind. But what lay ahead for them in the war-torn North? Would they find the rebels? And even if they did, would there be anyone among them who could help?

She looked up at Titus. 'We'll find her.'

'The four of us together?' he said, gesturing to her, Bramley and Thorn with a wave of his hand. 'I'd wager my life on it.'

EPILOGUE

Two weeks later . . .

John Stearne, the Witch Hunter General, grabbed his prisoner by the collar and pushed him through the door. 'Move yourself, I haven't got all day.'

Matthew Hopkins stumbled a few steps down the path, then tripped over the chain shackling his ankles. The sun was bright after the darkness of his cell, and when his eyes adjusted he saw soldiers tearing his garden apart – digging over the turf and tossing the plants and flowers he'd spent months nurturing on to a smouldering bonfire.

'Get up.' Stearne took a handful of Hopkins' shirt and hauled him to his feet.

Hopkins tried to keep his voice calm. 'You don't have to do this. I can help you . . .'

'Help?' Stearne let out a bark of laughter. 'From you? The man who let our greatest enemy escape? I think not.'

'Then why not let me go?' A touch of pique returned when he added, 'Dammit, John, it's just not *seemly* for a man like me to be treated this way.'

'All men are equal under my law,' Stearne growled, shoving him down the path. 'Your time is over, Hopkins. Mine is beginning, and I will bring down such a storm of vengeance on our enemies that they'll look back on your tenure as one of peace and benevolence.'

'Please, all I'm asking is that you let me go.'

They stopped by the Oven's metal hatch. Stearne wrenched it open to reveal the broiling darkness inside.

Hopkins began to tremble. 'I promise,' he said, 'you'll never hear from me again.'

A smile spread across Stearne's brutal face. 'I know.'

ABOUT THE AUTHOR

Matt Ralphs was born in North Lincolnshire and grew up in Kent. So, by way of a median average, he's from Cambridge. He now lives on a canal boat called *Nostromo* and is a full-time writer.

Fire Witch is his second novel.

ACKNOWLEDGEMENTS

I wrote my first book, *Fire Girl*, over the course of about five years, scribbling feverishly on my commute, during boring work meetings, and in the quiet of the night. I worked in the hope but not the expectation of one day getting it published; I had no deadline, no publisher's 'to-print date' – hence the leisurely gestation.

The writing of *Fire Witch* occurred at a comparatively breakneck speed. Just over a year from first draft to final layouts. The difference this time was that I knew the book was going to be published and I had the full backing of Macmillan Children's Books behind me. It's been brilliant.

Authors tend to get all the plaudits, but I used to work in publishing so I know how much hard labour and care comes from the many people behind the scenes. The sales, publicity and marketing teams, booksellers, designers and artists, typesetters, editorial assistants, managers, accountants, rights department, publishers and editors. Take a bow, y'all, and accept my heartfelt thanks.

Special mention simply must go to Rachel Kellehar, my awesome editor. Your faith and tireless effort on Hazel's behalf mean a lot to me. This book is yours as much as it is mine.